The Golden Dog Tag

Winifred Rowland with Wendy J. Woodcock

GW00569734

ISBN 9781916316942

Contents

Chapter 1

December 1938 - Crewe, North of England

'Mum! I think Dad's got another family. I've just seen him taking a lady and two kids to see Father Christmas.'

'No. Don't be daft.' Felicity said, putting down her romance novel.

'I know my own dad!' Anna said, as she unbuttoned her heavy tweed coat, yanked off a yellow woollen hat and ruffled out her thick auburn hair.

'Of course, you do. Where were you?'

'In Lewis's, paying for my dress pattern. They were queuing for Santa's Grotto but didn't see me.'

Felicity stomach churned as she wrestled with a shadowy, unwelcome veil of doom.

'He was carrying a little boy, and the lady was holding the girl. By the time I'd collected my change, they'd disappeared inside. It was getting dark, so I rode home.' Wide-eyed, the teenager looked at her mother for an explanation.

Felicity stood up, turned around and hung onto the cold pottery sink, her mind scrabbling for something coherent to say. With all the calmness she could muster, she said, 'Oh yes, I remember now. He was helping the wife of a workmate. Don't say anything; it might embarrass him.' Felicity hoped her quick thinking played for time while she assessed this bombshell.

Anna accepted the white lie, crossed to the pantry, and glanced over her shoulder. 'Strange though, the boy had red hair just like mine.' She opened the cake tin, selected a biscuit, and turned on the radio. 'Is Betsy upstairs reading again?'

Felicity thought, *'This can't be true. George said he was glad for the overtime. Time and a half on a Saturday.'*

Betsy heard her elder sister's voice, careered downstairs, and hurtled into the kitchen. 'Hi Anna, did you get your pattern? What's for dinner, Mum?'

'Stew and dumplings. Ready in ten minutes. You can set the table now.' The girls busied themselves, by throwing a gingham tablecloth over the wooden table and setting out the cutlery. They sat down to exchange their day's happenings, and Anna pulled out her pattern and material and handed them to Betsy.

Anna said, 'Now I'm working; I only get a couple of days off at Christmas and one for New Year.'

Betsy said, 'Ah, but you'll have money to go to the pictures and buy nice things.'

That response formed a truce, and they moved on to discuss festive ideas.

Over dinner, Felicity, unusually quiet, scrutinised George's everyday activities, now or in the past, for anything amiss or out of character. *He belongs to the Railwayman's Club, plays bowls in the summer and darts in the winter. He drinks the occasional beer, has the odd fag and comes home either smelling of engine oil or tobacco smoke. We're just a regular little family, busy with our pastimes. I can't think why he would deceive me.'*

The women moved to the living room. The girls were learning to knit, and Felicity had shown them how to read and follow a pattern. She looked up when the mantle clock chimed eight. *'He'll be home soon if he worked late. But was he working overtime or meeting another woman?'* Her heart sank. *'Now I've got to question everything he does.'*

She turned to the girls for distraction. 'How's the knitting coming on?'

Betsy looked up. 'Will you help me finish this scarf for next week? I want to give it to Emily as a Christmas present.'

While Felicity showed her how to knot the fringe, she mulled over further ramifications of Anna's discovery. *'I've trusted George all our married life. I never questioned his working hours or earnings. He handles all the money and gives me good housekeeping, leaving me plenty   for birthdays or Christmas.'*

4

Felicity jumped as George barged into the living room, rubbing his hands. 'It's ruddy cold out there.' He shrugged off his heavy winter coat and tweed cap, stepped into the kitchen, hung it on the hook behind the back door, and returned to the welcoming fireplace.

She checked what he was wearing; the usual weekend clothes, a jumper over a collared shirt. She closed her book, and as guilt swept up her cheeks, she looked away.

'Hot drink?' she asked casually.

'I do need a warm-up,' he said, standing with his back in front of the blazing fire. He glanced at the girls. They lifted their heads briefly and he nodded as Felicity placed the steaming mug of cocoa on the mantelpiece. He slumped in the worn leather armchair with the newspaper.

'You've eaten already?' She tried to get a whiff of oil or cigarette smoke from his clothes but smelt nothing and joined the girls at the colourful wool mountain strewn across the gate-leg table.

'Aye, grabbed a bite at the Club,' he said, fixing his eyes on the football results. After a few minutes, she suddenly felt uncomfortable sitting in oppressive silence while he read.

She peered over at him; *'He seems the same. I'm not sure what I expect to see. What does an adulterer look like?'* She couldn't settle and said, 'I've had a busy day. Early night for me.'

He grunted.

She added, 'Don't stay up too late, girls. Church in the morning.'

For a few days, Felicity watched and waited for anything unusual. George's morning ritual began early; he was always quiet as he dressed, not to awaken the girls. She pretended to be asleep but snatched furtive glances through half-closed eyes to see what he was wearing as he tiptoed out of the bedroom.

One night, she pretended to be asleep when he came home late. As she lay beside him, the heat of his body made her skin crawl. She rolled over towards her edge of the mattress, her back to him, giving him more room than usual. The unmistakable cloying odour of machine oil clung to his hair. He hadn't been to the club due to

5

the absence of beer or cigarette smell. Perhaps he really was working late.

Felicity had gaily trodden an easy life path; with no adverse setbacks. Her contentment was in jeopardy; turmoil now tossed her world without compunction. Lacking confirmation of his infidelity, she couldn't confide in anyone. She struggled to find any solace in the insecurity of her position.

That week, fitful rest was all she could manage, often awake with bubbling anger. *'How long has this been going on?'* She loathed the silent sleeping body beside her, hated him for this ultimate betrayal. *'Which is more despicable, the time or money George spends on his other family?'*

She ignored the mounting pressure, trying to get off the seesaw of beliefs vacillating between *'This is ridiculous,* and *'What if it's true?'* She couldn't stem the persistent fear and foreboding slithering through her mind. *'Should I do something? How can I confirm what Anna saw?'* She knew, if validated, it could rock her and her family's world forever, change everything she believed they had.

When Anna said, 'Mum, you're looking drawn. Is everything alright?' That was the final straw. *'I can't live like this. I have to find out.'*

One sentence still haunted her: *'I think Dad's got another family.'*

Chapter 2

Felicity chose the following Saturday to execute her plan. Everything else was unimportant. She wandered around the grocery shops in a state of mental anguish, unable to focus on anything apart from her afternoon excursion. It had taken all her willpower not to challenge George during the week. She took a crowded, smoke-filled train to Nantwich, the small town five miles from Crewe, a fifteen-minute ride away.

She remembered seeing a second-storey cafe with a commanding view over the High Street, perfect for her purpose. It was a short walk from the station, and she was pleased she wore a headscarf and boots, which protected her from the icy blast.

In the warm cafe, with two battered wooden stools against the counter, the shopkeeper checked the appetising cakes and bread displayed in the window. A handwritten sign showed "More Seating for Tea and Coffee", with an arrow pointing upstairs. When Felicity entered, she glanced up from serving cakes, shouted, 'Tea?' and pointed to the sign. Felicity nodded. 'Won't be a moment.'

Felicity slowly walked up the stairs. The room held four small tables and chairs. Alone, she chose a table away from the vast windows. She looked to see if it had the viewpoint she needed. The pavement was widened by a curve, leading to a parade of shops.

Nantwich was a quaint town with original black and white Tudor-timbered houses and shops. Most specialised in just one line of goods.

Felicity analysed her situation. *'What if he doesn't show up? Am I being stupid? How could he possibly have another family and keep it hidden?'* She rose to her feet, grabbed her bag, and dismissed this visit as dramatic nonsense.

Before she reached the stairs, the shop assistant met her with a tray with a white cup and saucer, a pot of tea and a tiny jug of cold milk. Felicity felt obliged to stay and slumped back into her seat. The shopkeeper looked at the busy street below and glanced sideways to see if this mute, tense customer was a regular but didn't recognise her.

Felicity shakily poured the tea and looked down to the street below, trying to spot a neat family of four within the hubbub. Before she had finished the cup, her heart leapt as a group stopped and drew to one side while the mother consulted her shopping list. The little girl held onto the father's hand as he leaned forward over the pushchair and teased the child. This man was achingly familiar; she knew every inch of his tall, muscular body; it was George.

The girl took hold of the pushchair handle as he lifted the little auburn-haired boy. Felicity stared in disbelief; she couldn't take her eyes off the touching domestic scene. The woman was an ordinary-looking housewife. Her dark fringe poked out beneath a bright silk scarf. Within seconds, the happy family vignette crawled out of her vision like a slow-motion picture.

The tableau repeatedly played in Felicity's mind like a faulty projector. Her hands trembled as she picked up her tea, amazed it was still hot. In three minutes, her life had crumbled. Somebody had blown a starting whistle, and the train of events was gathering speed.

She gripped the banister as she walked in a daze downstairs and fumbled for change to pay the shopkeeper. The chilly wind whipped her face, and she turned her collar up as she marched to the train station, and anger replaced bewilderment. *'George never displayed that depth of warmth and caring towards our children. How many lies had he told to maintain his double life? He must have thought I was gullible.'* Bitterness kept her company as she watched the fields roll by. *'Has he told her about the girls and me? I doubt it.'*

The shock lingered for days. Felicity often wanted to shake the sleeping body next to her and talk things through but silently considered her options. There was nothing to gain. She could follow him but had no appetite for being a spy. The sordid dreariness, dragging the girls into it, was depressing, and she rejected that course of action. She wished her supportive Auntie Mabel lived nearer.

Chapter 3

Auntie Mabel was Felicity's mother's sister, a spinster in her late fifties. She had been instrumental in helping Felicity sort out her parents' belongings after they died in the same year. Her father from a heart attack, and her mother from pancreatic cancer, weakened by a flu outbreak. Felicity moved in with Mabel, and the shared resources and company were helpful to both women until she married George.

Mabel's fiancé died during the First World War. They didn't need him for active service; he was too old at twenty-nine, with poor eyesight, but being a farmhand, he desperately wanted to help horses in the war zone. He volunteered and was recruited to the farrier's role, taking horses onto the battlefield. This robust and lone figure picked his way amongst the dying or maimed bodies with a horse and cart, searching for any sign of life or reason to be loaded onto this ramshackle wooden platform.

The death of a horse, usually protected by leather armour, was a bitter defeat, and he resorted to pushing a wheelbarrow to collect the injured. When the wheelbarrow gave out, his weary shoulders took the strain on these ultimate missions of mercy.

Unfortunately, wandering about the battlefield made him an easy target for the enemy sharpshooters, and a quick death rewarded him for his bravery. The First World War wiped out an entire generation of young men. Many who survived came home gassed or shell-shocked at the horrors they had witnessed.

Mabel felt bitter about his death because he didn't have to go. They dreamed of being tenants on a small farm after years of careful saving. There was little chance of her meeting anyone else due to the loss of so many men.

Some good came out of the hostilities; women deputising for men at war became natural successors. No longer were they little ladies tending to household chores and children. They could work and make money.

Mabel Evans was used to hard work; she began as a schoolgirl washing glasses and bottles after school and at weekends in a public house in the centre of Crewe. When she left school, she automatically took this job full-time. Tall, strong and unshockable, able to handle the chancers. For twenty years, she moved from pubs to better-paid jobs in working men's clubs catering to the railway workers in this vital rail network hub in the Midlands.

Mr Davies, one of her regulars, a traveller from Cardiff to Manchester, always stopped off for a pint and a pie as he changed trains. In his middle fifties, clean-shaven, brown hair plastered back neatly, he looked smart in his Crombie overcoat and leather gloves. He sat on a stool at the end of the bar, and before long, Mabel's boss signalled her to join them.

'I'll come straight to the point, Mabel,' Mr Davies said. 'How do you fancy working in Manchester? I own the big pub by the market, The Duke of Wellington, now known as The Wellington. Do you know it?'

Mabel nodded vigorously. 'Yes, I've been in a couple of times. It's always busy. Do you really want to hire someone over fifty?'

'That's not a problem. I'd like you to be the manageress, in charge of everything. I want to leave it with someone reliable and experienced, allowing me to follow other interests. You'll have full power to fire and hire as needed.' As an enticement, he added, 'It's a huge responsibility and will command the appropriate wage.'

'I'll take it!' she said without hesitation.

'In which case, you'll need somewhere to stay, and I can rent you my house for a while. We want to leave the noise and smoke. Our place will sell eventually at a profit when the rebuilding starts around there. You'll be doing me a favour by keeping an eye on it and overseeing any maintenance. Have you any questions?'

She said, 'Can you tell me more about the running of the pub?'

'Maggie currently deals with that. It's a tradition to open early to catch the stallholders after they've set up. They love a big mug of thick soup and a chunk of crusty bread to keep them going. We then open officially to the public at eleven.'

He pulled on his leather gloves, 'Why not come to Manchester on Saturday, and you can see the whole caboodle, meet the staff, and you'll soon see whether it's for you?'

'Yes, I will. What time shall we meet?' This new prospect excited Mabel.

'After lunch, say one-thirty. You can come over, see the house and meet my wife.'

'Alright. I'll see you on Saturday.' Mabel confirmed.

Her current boss came over and, noting her shocked, ashen face, said, 'I know what he's just asked you. Why don't you leave early? Perhaps go over and discuss it with George and Felicity. I've known Mr Davies for years, and I can vouch for him. Don't worry about me. Of course, I'll miss you, but you're perfect for that job, just what he needs there.'

Mabel took the next bus to Felicity's and George's house. They were surprised to see her at dinner time. 'I've been offered a job and digs in Manchester, managing a pub in the city centre. It's big with a lively, busy atmosphere. I'm a bit overwhelmed, but I've scheduled to check it out on Saturday.'

Felicity's eyes widened with disbelief at her aunt leaving Crewe. She wanted to seem supportive and said, 'It seems like a fantastic opportunity, and you'll only be an hour away. Why don't I go with you, see the set-up, and do some shopping? While you're here, fancy staying for beef stew? We've got plenty to go round.'

That weekend, Felicity and Mabel giggled like two naughty teenagers as the Crewe train arrived in Manchester's city centre. Felicity had never seen a market on such a vast scale and walked in awe as stallholders finished their colourful, sometimes exotic, displays. They recoiled at the sight of game birds, either dead or alive. The cheeping of day-old chicks peeping out of air holes in cardboard boxes attracted the passing children. One of them gazed hungrily at the mound of polished apples and suddenly heard "catch" as an apple came hurtling through the air towards him from an amused stallholder.

Beyond the open market, a man in blue and white striped overalls hung carcasses on hooks and sprinkled sawdust on the stone flags at a butcher's shop.

Traditionally, stallholders marked down anything unsold before closing time or donated perishable goods to the poor, grateful refugees living in the ghettos and hovels of Red Bank down by the river.

After gazing around the department stores, they reached the olde-worlde pub by midday. It was thriving with shoppers rummaging through their store bags, revelling in their bargain purchases and nursing their weary feet. In a quiet moment, Mabel introduced herself to the barman; he said they expected Mr Davies within the hour, which gave them time to have lunch. They dunked their bread in the famous soup while taking in the lively scene, listening in wonderment at the salesman shouting their tempting pitches outside.

Mabel then asked the bartender if she could take a quick look in the kitchen. After ten minutes, she returned to Felicity with a big smile. 'It's all so clean, and the staff are welcoming. I think I'll like it here. I've ordered us coffee to celebrate.'

Felicity clapped with excitement at her aunt's prospect of a new city life. Mr Davies strode in and waved to the barman, who pointed to Mabel at the window table. He pulled up a chair.

'This is Felicity, my niece,' Mabel said.

'Nice to meet you, Felicity. I've heard only good things about your Aunt Mabel; she'll fit in just right. She's what this place needs.' She immediately warmed to his gentle language and enthusiasm.

He turned to Mabel. 'I've got us a lift to my house at Ardwick Green. Don't be misled by the name,' he joked. 'There's not much greenery hereabouts. We live just behind it. My wife's dying to meet you and invites you to tea.'

From Mr Davies's showy clothes and air of opulence, it startled Mabel when a warm, homely lady in a blowsy dress topped by a white apron opened the door. She said, 'Pleased to meet you. Let me show you around and see if the house suits you.'

Mabel knew straight away the house was perfect. Its front steps and porch gave it an air of importance. It was also very near to the city for her commute.

Mrs Davies said, 'We have three bedrooms and a bathroom upstairs. Sid, our handyman, will freshen the paintwork and would like to start next week, if that's okay? What do you think about the pub?'

'It seems perfect to me, and I'm grateful to rent your lovely house.'

Mr Davies chimed in, 'Some regulars are rough but as good as gold. When the offices shut down, business slows. A few stragglers may call in, so we clean around them, and you'll be able to finish early.'

Mrs Davies showed off the large backyard and luxury of a tap and secondary lavatory outside.

Mabel felt overwhelmed at the size of the house but excited at her luck landing a prized job and a lovely home to match. It would serve her well up to retirement.

After tasting a few tiny delicate sandwiches and scrumptious homemade scones, Mr Davies took Mabel aside to discuss remuneration and rent. Felicity could see Mabel nodding at all he proposed and knew it was full steam ahead.

He brought his little car around to drive them to the station. They made good time against the evening rush-hour traffic, with crocodiles of buses crammed with workers bound for homes in the suburbs.

Once settled in the train carriage, Felicity and Mabel linked arms, lost in their own thoughts. There was nothing to discuss; as Mabel's new boss said, 'A once-in-a-lifetime offer.'

Chapter 4

After her husband left for work, Felicity sat up in bed and pondered, *'Why, George? Why did I marry him? Did I have an instant attraction to him? No.He was nothing special, stocky, with sandy hair, hazel-flecked eyes and a slight dusting of freckles across his cheeks.'*

She had just turned nineteen, still grieving from the loss of her parents and he was attentive and easy company. His father had also died young, so he became a sympathetic ally.

In their small group of friends, they were quieter and more serious, so it was natural they teamed up. When he proposed, everyone considered him a good match for her because he had a trade in train engineering which paid well.

George appeared to have a cushy number, living at home with his mother, Ethel, spoiling him. He proved them wrong because, after a six-month engagement, he couldn't wait to enter the independence and serenity of marriage with Felicity.

She appealed to him, a pleasant-looking, fair-haired girl who seemed confident and non-confrontational. When someone at the railway offered him a house to rent, he was quick to take it and get married, relieved to escape his dominant mother.

Ethel was a dynamic character, organising good works in and out of the church. Tall, white wavy hair and a sunny, smiling disposition that brooked no opposition, convinced Our Lord was always with her. She was a part-time shop assistant with a widow's pension, and to keep the family home after George left, she rented out rooms, mainly for the income but also she needed the company.

Over the years, Felicity hoped his demeanour would lighten up as the children grew, but it didn't. He became more introverted and answered in monosyllables.

She refused to see Anna and Betsy stifled by their non-communicative father and encouraged them to have interesting conversations over dinner. He never seemed interested or laughed at their daily antics, and they soon learned not to bother him more than that with their banter.

As Felicity made the bed she thought, *'He was never demonstrative in public and hardly showed affection to me behind closed doors. At least he didn't beat me like some of the horror stories I've heard from the churchwomen.*

She picked up the post from the door, *'I'd love to confide in someone, but I don't know the truth. It's hard to believe, but has married life always been a mundane charade for him?'*

Chapter 5

The previous summer, outside the hardware shop in Nantwich, George fatefully first set eyes on Polly. It was a stifling Saturday afternoon, and his mission was to order a monkey wrench for work.

He stopped to let a woman cross the road, who angled a pushchair onto the pavement in front of him. Her foot slipped back, and a white high heel slid into the roadside metal grid. As it wedged, she fell forward, and he automatically grabbed her arm with one hand and steadied the pushchair with the other.

She lurched out of the shoe, and ungainly stepped onto the paving. George bent down to wriggle the shoe out of the grating. He wobbled the sad broken heel and handed it to the woman.

With a rare laugh, he said, 'Look! Luckily, we're outside a shoe shop. You can buy some cheap slippers here. Otherwise, I'd have to carry you home.'

She laughed at his joke with the bent heel wobbling in her hand. Her perfectly straight teeth lit up an ethereal face. Mesmerised, he secretly devoured her blue eyes and luxurious dark brown hair. He had never seen such beauty, which forced him to stay and talk. 'Don't struggle with the children; I'll look after them while you nip into the shop. What are their names?'

At first, Polly wasn't sure. *'Could she hand her beloved screamers to a stranger? But he's right; it would be quicker.'*

'They are Jean and Bertie. You're not going to run off with them, are you?' she said, partly in jest.

'No. I've already got two,' George tried to look fatherly and harmless. 'Oh, and my name's George.'

'If you're sure. Thank you. I won't be a moment.' She stayed near the window to monitor them and sported her new plimsolls with pride when she skipped outside.

She tucked the change in her pocket, 'Thank you very much for your help. I feel silly breaking my shoe like that. I must let you get on.'

He nodded and racked his brains, groping for any excuse to extend the conversation. 'I'm here to pick up a monkey wrench' was the only banal phrase he could muster. He longed to blurt out, *'Who are you, you gorgeous being? I want to know everything about you.'*

'We're off to do our shopping. Thanks once again.' She gathered the two children and set off towards the greengrocers.

He fantasized about her all the way home on the train. *'What's happening to me? She sets me on fire. Stupid man, I didn't even get her name.'*

George strolled into the house and shouted. No answer; nobody was at home yet, which pleased him. He wanted to prolong and wallow in his newfound feelings. *'I just want to touch her, but she's probably married.'* He read the note on the kitchen table. *"School concert. Dinner in the oven. Cake in the tin."* He looked around at the clean, welcoming house. *'It's Saturday; I'll have a beer.'*

As he lifted the bottle opener, it hit him that his home life was dull and mediocre. *'Felicity is the perfect undemanding wife. We're fond of each other; that's good enough. Or is it? I have stronger feelings about a stranger I've talked to for five minutes than my wife of sixteen years.'*

During the working week, the unknown woman's face constantly tantalised George. He recalled her black lashes against the sweep of her cheekbones as she looked down at her children. Her eyes had a depth enhanced by a tinge of violet. He had only met her for a few moments, but by Friday, he decided to return and try to 'accidentally' bump into her. He presumed she wouldn't be shopping for provisions on a Saturday unless she worked.

He often lost concentration and produced half-baked work while dreaming of possessing her. He wallowed in his fantasies, ordinary from anyone else's viewpoint. The whole scenario intrigued him, and he imagined how to engineer future meetings. *'How can I approach her? I'd feel stupid if she snubbed me. Ah, I can source a replacement part.'*

The following day, George casually strolled Nantwich High Street around the same time as last week. *'Why do I long to see her again? This mad attraction has never happened to me before.'* He clenched and unclenched his hands, but he didn't have long to wait. When the object of his desire came into view, he gave an involuntary sigh of relief.

Polly held her shopping list, and the little girl, Jean, was swinging the empty shopping bag. Bertie entertained himself by kicking his legs against the pushchair.

George had butterflies but was ready for the encounter. He nonchalantly brushed past her in the street, but she didn't see him. However, the little girl recognised the stranger she'd seen the week before and shouted, 'Hello, mister.'

Polly looked back and saw George looking rather splendid in a sports jacket. She almost didn't recognise him out of his overalls.

George quickly lied, 'Hello again, the replacement part will be ready for collection in half an hour.'

She raised her eyebrows, 'I'm doing the usual boring grocery shopping.'

He brought his bravery to the fore. 'Perhaps you have time for a cup of tea. I could buy Bertie and Jean ice cream?'

On hearing their names and the word 'ice cream', Jean forced the issue by pulling George's hand towards the tea shop. Bertie looked pleadingly at his mum until she gave in. Polly said, 'Okay, I can spare fifteen minutes. By the way, my name is Polly.'

They ordered a pot of tea. It was a treat for Polly to relax and unburden herself. 'My husband was a Londoner, a railway engineer transferred to Crewe and killed in a fall. Being independent is difficult and raising two kids alone is hard. My family's keen to help me, but I'm staying away from their help as long as possible.'

She had been so frank about her situation and the death of her young husband; George wanted to reciprocate. He had rehearsed being non-committal and dull when regaling his life story, but as he looked into her eyes, he blurted out his background, wanting her to understand everything about him.

'I have a disjointed life with my wife and two teenage daughters. We speak different languages; they gossip endlessly about school projects, lesson preparation, and people I've never met.'

Polly held her cup of tea in both hands and nodded.

Encouraged by the full beam of her attention, 'I'm an engineer and work long hours, so I put my feet up, relax, and let their female chatter sail over my head when I get home. I gave up listening when I couldn't remember their teachers' names every year. I should have tried harder, but I'd lost interest. It might have been different if I'd had sons rather than daughters. I'm a bit like an alien at home.'

He shocked himself with this impassioned speech. *'Have I told her too much already? Will it scare her off?'*

His outpouring was heartfelt, and she sympathetically placed her delicate hand over his and squeezed it. It was not the usual "*my wife doesn't understand me*" cliche. Comically, just the opposite. She watched his eyes sparkle with indignation, with a slight tremble of his lips, and gave him an understanding smile. She thought, *'You are not an alien, someone to be side-lined. With some luck, you're a strong, virile man who will soon become my playmate. Widowhood is lonely, frustrating and no joke. We need each other at this moment.'*

She tried not to behave like a wanton, waiting to be set free, and smirked when her mind playfully suggested, *'I'll make sure he won't forget this teacher's name.'*

He watched, fascinated, as her face became more animated as she relayed her story. 'I was an infant teacher before I married. It was easy to earn a living here in a creche to be near my two children.'

With a firm voice, he nodded emphatically. 'You're brilliant, how you cope and plan. Indeed, the two youngsters are a credit to you. You should be very proud.'

She blushed and looked down at Bertie, who had the auburn colouring of his father, and then over at Jean, who'd inherited her brunette locks.

George wanted to stay longer but forced himself to look at his watch. Not wanting to outstay his welcome, he got up to pay the bill. As he walked across the cafe, her eyes followed his long, athletic strides, and she noticed his muscular arms and strong thighs. She gave a deep sigh, brought back into sharp focus by two sets of child's eyes waiting for instructions.

'Right, kids. We're off now. Did you enjoy your ice-creams? Say thank you to the nice gentleman.'

Jean smiled at him and said, 'Thank you, mister', as George returned to the table.

He couldn't invent a way to prolong the meeting with this scintillating woman and her enchanting children. He looked into her eyes. 'Thank you for keeping me company. I hope we can do this again soon.'

'Yes, that would be nice.'

'Perhaps next week? About the same time?' he tried to be cool and inwardly pleaded for her to respond "Yes".

'I'll look forward to it,' she purred.

He opened the door, lifted the pushchair over the wooden threshold onto the pavement, and lingered outside the cafe, his heart pounding, watching their every movement until the little family was out of sight.

She had hooked him and purposefully didn't look back.

George lived for the following Saturday, although many times he wavered. *'I must stop this. I will not go again.'* But the week dragged and he couldn't bear it if he didn't see her just once more. Compelled, he caught the afternoon train.

Polly lingered outside the cafe, and her face lit up when she saw George striding toward them. The children jumped along the pavement to welcome him, and four little hands dragged him inside by his trousers.

They ordered two coffees and strawberry ice cream as a treat for the children. Their smiles widened at their clandestine meeting as they sat opposite each other. She looked different. A dab of lipstick and a hint of perfume made her irresistible as she took off her cardigan, and he could glimpse her slender frame.

After glossing over many topics, they finally found common ground in raising children. She said, 'Don't your family miss you?'

He laughed aloud and, in a mock severe voice, said, 'Good heavens, no! They are very busy people.'

After fifteen minutes of general banter and arranging to meet at the park next week, he waited in the queue to pay the bill. He looked around, but they had left. As he stepped outside, they waved at him from across the road. He exaggerated his nod to them and gradually walked in the opposite direction. He enjoyed a beer in the nearest pub to prolong the thrill of the day.

The following Saturday, George met Polly at the gate to the kiddies' park. He bought ice-creams, and then the children rushed over to the swings. On a wooden bench, Polly edged nearer and nearer to George until they touched, pressing their shoulders, thighs and feet against each other. The heat of desire sizzled through their clothes; they dared not look sideways at each other for fear of breaking the spell.

She said, 'I nearly didn't come today; I was waiting for a plumber to fix a leak in the lavatory, but he didn't show.'

He looked at her, knowing he was leaning towards the forbidden territory. 'Good gracious! You shouldn't be paying for a plumber when I can do it. You live near here, you said?' He didn't want to seem too eager.

She nodded. 'I have tools at home, but they may not be right for the job.'

'I'll take a look anyway?'

'OK. Shall we go now?

They walked the few minutes to her home, much to the delight of Jean and Bertie. She rented a small two-up-two-down terraced house with a tiny kitchen that led into the yard.

He fixed the leak temporarily. 'I'll be over tomorrow with the right tools to repair it properly. It should hold until then.'

Polly saw an opportunity. 'If you come around midday, you can join us for lunch.'

'I'd like that.' George inwardly berated himself for readily accepting, '*How am I going to explain this to Felicity?*'

She saw him out as the tots ate their tea. He brushed past her as he made for the front door, tempted to touch her, but dared not risk it. '*This was a lucky break, don't spoil it,*' he thought.

George woke early, agitated about his impending visit to Polly. After making porridge and toast, he glanced at the Sunday paper headlines several times, but his mind kept wandering. '*How can I tell them I won't be here for lunch?*'

21

Felicity and the girls chatted noisily in the hallway, ready for the short walk to church. She glanced around the lounge door to say goodbye and looked over at George, surprised he was wearing overalls over his smart shirt.

'It's Sunday. Are you working today?'

He said casually, 'Doing a plumbing job for a mate; I owe him one. He'll probably give me Sunday lunch.'

'That's nice of him,' she said, trying not to sound sarcastic. 'You could've given me more notice, but it means more roast beef for us, doesn't it, girls?'

George's cheeks reddened, and he lifted the newspaper, hoping the heat from his lying face didn't penetrate it.

When they had gone, he marched to the station for the next train to Nantwich and bounded to Polly's house. She was in a floral shirtwaister dress and white cardigan and greeted him with a kiss. After soldering the pipe joint outside, he wriggled free of his overalls and was ready to join them for roast lamb.

'This looks tasty,' he said, eyeing the big slices she cut. He smiled at the children, who crowded around to see him again, and asked if he'd brought ice cream. He shook his head but produced two small bars of chocolate from his trouser pocket, which he'd bought at the station.

After lunch, Polly's neighbour collected the children for afternoon Sunday School, leaving Polly with more than an hour to 'deal with the plumber'. The moment the door closed behind them, Polly took the initiative and led him by the hand, unfastening the few front buttons on her summer dress as she sauntered upstairs. George's legs shook as he stumbled behind her. She hadn't been wearing underclothes.

On that visit, he noticed nothing about the bedroom, only her thin body framed by the smooth blue counterpane, which echoed her violet eyes. Her arms were wide and welcoming. Her animated face gave away her longing and excitement as she impatiently watched him wrenching at his clothes. She sighed when, at last, their lips touched, and she melted around him.

It was thrilling to welcome a man into her arms. His strength as he lifted her nearer, the muscles and the smell of him

22

overwhelmed her into complete submission. Her active, demanding participation delighted George, his relations with his wife had no bells or whistles.

She caressed his cheek, slid off the bed, dressed shyly, knowing he was watching and thought, *'You've got a lot to learn, Mr Plumber! But you'll be an eager pupil.'* A smile developed, and he grinned in response.

They were drinking warm tea and luxuriating in post-coital languor in the living room when the shrieking intrusive chatter of the children spoiled it. This grated on his newfound bliss. He looked at his watch and made an excuse to leave.

Polly's thoughts were dominant enough to cut out the kids' prattle, *'Perhaps I don't need to return South just yet! I was getting bored with this quiet provincial life, but it's spicing up a bit now. Like a perfect holiday, he must learn that planning, anticipation, and the journey are often as thrilling as arriving at the destination.'*

As he was leaving, she asked Jean, 'Is it next Sunday morning when your junior choir is giving a concert? Perhaps we can all have lunch later?' She spoke to the child but looked at George; her eyebrows lifted slightly; thus, a pattern formed.

George mulled over the consequences of taking another Sunday away from the family. He had to ensure his excuses sounded genuine. The truth was a good start; he had been fixing a toilet.

Few men were in Polly's and her children's lives, and a relationship with George developed rapidly. His passion for their mother encompassed her children. It was a novelty to have a surrogate son. Bertie cuddled up to him, constantly vying to get his exclusive attention. George experienced more enrichment and comfort at their humble house as the months passed.

Occasionally, he popped in after work for the children's bedtime story, knowing they would be asleep within minutes and he would have stolen time with Polly. He'd never practised deception, which added frisson to the affair and carried on into the winter.

Chapter 6

Felicity lay motionless by George's body and only managed a couple of hours of sleep as her mind swirled around her predicament. She'd decided not to destroy the family Christmas as they were well on with festive preparations, and she was fearful about the future.

She ventured downstairs at nine o'clock in a heavy skirt and jumper against the icy cold. The fire in the living room soon let warm air permeate the kitchen.

In the living room were piles of unopened boxes and bags of donated provisions, ribbons and wrappings. Tomorrow, Betsy would take on a labour of love and bake mince pies and shortbread biscuits for the gift boxes. Other churchgoers would add tangerines, nuts, and chocolate to cheer up the needy or solitary parishioners.

Mentally and physically, she shook herself like a sopping dog. This terrible secret might ruin her Christmas, but she'll ensure nothing spoils it for the girls. It would be sensible and less traumatic to leave the decision-making until after the festivities.

She fastened her blue velour coat, pulled on her woolly hat and hurried to the grocery store for vegetables to accompany the evening's dinner.

A dog darting out of the shop door shook Felicity out of her misery. It shot across the pavement towards the road. She sidestepped heavily on the dog's lead in a swift automatic movement, pulling it up abruptly. A second later, 'whoosh'; a car drove past, missing his head by inches. She breathed out heavily and reeled him in by his lead. She bent down to the mongrel, 'You're one lucky dog. That's what you are, really lucky.'

The dog's owner stood white and open-mouthed in the shop doorway. 'Oh, my goodness. Thank God you were there. Rover would've been killed.'

Felicity handed the brown terrier back but saw the lady struggling to contain the long lead, a shopping bag and a walking stick. She recognised her as a fellow churchgoer, and they exchanged pleasantries on the way out.

'I'll walk you back if you like. Do you live far?' and Felicity gently took the dog. 'Mrs Jones, isn't it?'

She nodded. 'I can't thank you enough. I'm Carol; I live just five minutes along the street.' She pointed to her bandaged foot. 'It's just a sprain, but such a nuisance. I'm supposed to be resting it.'

'I'm Felicity. Haven't I seen you at our church services with your family?'

'Yes, that's right. You have two lovely girls. Have you time for a cup of tea?'

Glad for the diversion, Felicity accepted and helped Carol onto the step and into the hallway. They settled at the kitchen table with their mugs of tea while Carol put her foot on a stool and told her sorry tale.

'My husband, Stan, and the two boys are spending Christmas in Rhyll with my mother. I can't be with them this year; Rover would terrorise their two new cats.'

Felicity had a brilliant idea. She stated firmly, 'If Rover's is the only thing stopping you, he can spend Christmas with us. We haven't any pets, so the girls will spoil him rotten.'

Carol looked into this kind lady's sparkling eyes. Rover would be in capable hands. The thoughts of a lonely Christmas filled her with dread. 'If it's really alright with you. I'd love to go.'

Felicity looked at her watch. 'Scribble a note to Stan that you'll join them after all and ask him to meet you at Rhyll station tomorrow afternoon. I can catch the post on my way home. My daughter Betsy and I will pick up Rover at about nine tomorrow morning and see you on the train. Leave it all to me.'

Carol perked up. 'You're so kind. It'll be for five days, though. Will that be OK?'

'Stay as long as you like. We'll enjoy having a dog around the place. Now, where's your suitcase? Top of the wardrobe, I expect?'

'Yes. In the bedroom upstairs to the left. Please put it on the spare bed so I can start packing?' Carol's face brightened as she contemplated her impromptu holiday with the family, not to mention her husband's delight, who was not good at small talk with the in-laws.

Felicity wagged a finger, 'Don't bring it down. I'll do that tomorrow.'

Carol's delight was infectious, and Felicity walked back, uplifted, determined to make a good Christmas holiday for her girls and Rover!

The following day, she and Betsy returned to collect Rover. The plan had worked like clockwork, but Carol hesitated in the kitchen.

'Is there something else?' asked Felicity, not wanting her offer of help to backfire or lose this chance of a diversion from anxiety.

'I hate to impose, but could you collect the hen's eggs each day? Keep them, of course. A neighbour will feed them.' She pointed to a cardboard box on the kitchen sideboard. 'Take them; they're fresh today. They'll be useful over the holidays.'

Betsy peered out of the back door; she laughed at the six hens strutting along the makeshift wire run in the yard. She clipped the tan leather lead onto Rover's collar, inserted her hand through the loop, and picked up the handles of the giant cloth bag. Wedged carefully inside were the precious box of eggs, a rolled-up little dog quilt, bowls, and a brush in case he got muddy.

She smiled. *'Our neighbourhood dogs will stand back in amazement at this shiny miniature brown pig. The girls can decide what his doggie Christmas present can be.'*

Felicity picked up the suitcase and took hold of Carol's arm. She helped her out of the front door, locked up and pocketed the spare key. Carefree banter filled the street as the three cheerful women strolled along the pavement to the station.

On Christmas Eve, George came home from work early, threw his cap on the chair and announced, 'Three whole days at home. I am not moving from this fire. I'll get through my pile of old newspapers.' He poured himself a celebratory glass of pale ale and sank into his old brown leather easy chair.

Rover seized the chance, jumped onto his knee, and settled down. George stroked the new tenant's wiry fur.

'That's it. I can't move now,' he joked as he picked up his glass, stared into the flames, and relaxed.

Felicity's mouth gaped. *'Was this gentle, funny man the same hideous monster who'd occupied her mind the past two weeks?'* This confusion was a cruel trick of fate.

Christmas was always busy for Felicity and the girls. They distributed gift boxes to local pensioners, sang carols at church, and ate too many mince pies and iced fruit cake. While Felicity stumbled through the motions of a joyous festive period, her mind could not rest, knowing she had to face reality in the New Year.

On Christmas morning, the family visited George's mother to exchange gifts and have a mince pie. They didn't linger as Ethel was keen to attend her church. She loved Christmas and, after the morning carol service, helped serve the pensioners with a traditional steaming hot Christmas lunch. It was not a chore but gratifying to see their cheerful faces and join in their treat.

The family walked back in the chilly air and were glad to be home. Anna had previously prepared the carrots, sprouts, and potatoes for lunch. Felicity peeked into the oven at the slow cooking, basted turkey and made a separate stuffing. Betsy set the living room table with bright red napkins and sang along to carols playing on the wireless.

George, at the head of the table, made a big theatrical show using the carving knife and sharpening iron. Afterwards, they tucked into the festive meal, wore the paper hats from the pulled crackers, and traditionally left the gifts and mottos until the end of the meal.

He pointed to Rover lying in his easy chair. 'He's not staying there.' The little dog was puffing, shuddering and snoring.

Anna said, 'We're not to feed dogs turkey.' Betsy looked alarmed and guilty, and George laughed, pinched his nose, 'Time will tell.' It made Betsy shriek.

Felicity said, 'Mrs Jones needn't have worried about leaving her beloved pet. He's lapping up the attention, and her eggs have come in useful.'

George said, 'As usual, a splendid Christmas lunch.'

Felicity smiled quizzically at him. *'Is this really a compliment from someone who's betraying me?'*

27

Everyone volunteered to wash up, but Felicity allowed them to clear the table. 'I need to move to help the dinner settle.' She wanted to be alone. Throughout the dinner, George seemed to enjoy play-acting; he usually immersed himself in all the rituals of Christmas. There was nothing to suggest his thoughts were elsewhere.

George didn't know she knew his secret. Uncovering his deception less than a month before, Felicity had been begrudgingly catapulted from dutiful housewife to detective.

Before New Year, the Jones family reclaimed Rover. He half-heartedly greeted them, reluctantly let them put his lead on and had to be dragged out of the door, slowly leaving his comfortable holiday home. The two boys bombarded Felicity with stories of beach exploits and mountain climbing. Thankfully, even though it was winter, it had been sunny.

Stan Jones said to Felicity. 'Thanks a lot. Anything you want, just ask. Carol can walk much better now; it's been a real tonic for her.'

To take their mind off Rover's departure, Felicity and the girls sat around the living room table, wrapped tissues around their precious baubles and placed them carefully in a shoebox ready for the loft.

Over the next few weeks, militancy replaced Felicity's hurt and anger. With time on her side, she could play George's game, and having seen his hand, she could take advantage and beat him.

She and the girls had done nothing to warrant his betrayal. In her world, it was usual for the wronged wife to carry on while he appeared to outsiders to be the dutiful husband and father rather than a lord and master with a hidden dirty secret.

At home, his cheery demeanour all week unnerved Felicity. He paid her more attention than usual and still wanted his Friday night husbandly performance. As she lay there, *'Strange,'* she thought, *'It takes the anticipation of seeing another woman to bring him closer to me.'*

There had never been cause to analyse their intimate married life; it was routine. Extreme passion in romance books and films was a myth, not real life, at least not in hers. She couldn't remember when they stopped kissing each other goodbye. It gradually tailed off. The gesture meant nothing to them, an expected fake expression, such as 'Goodnight, sleep well.'

Inevitably, her tears secretly flowed. She may forgive a fling, but not a double life. His actions posed a dangerous threat to their daughters' stability, and self-preservation set in. She felt compelled to leave, but was it possible?

Over the next few days, she considered several ways to start a new life without him, but with no money behind her, every option led her to the Public Assistance Institution and a bleak future for herself and the girls. She was only in her mid-thirties and entirely capable of working, so she chose to bide her time. An adequate escape fund might take years to accumulate, but it could start with small economies in household expenses.

George worked long hours and again on some weekends. She had previously lauded and praised his diligence, but now, the word dalliance might be nearer the truth.

As she warmed the teapot, more questions arose. *'George hadn't mentioned work or invented plumbing emergencies for a sneaky getaway to see "his other family". Had he taken presents to the children beforehand, and why did he stay away from them all Christmas?'*

While she poured the hot water, her conscience told her to stop punishing herself and let go of this daily turmoil. With George's double life unearthed, her only option was to get away. The girls' happiness and well-being were paramount to her decision, and she'd brought them up to be capable and withstand adversity. Satisfied with her intention to leave, Felicity was uplifted, ready to intensify her money-making activities, but what more could she do?

Outside the butchers, her mind returned to her meagre shopping list. A familiar little dog jumping around and dragging his lead in circles around her ankles interrupted her.

In her lilting Welsh voice, Carol said, 'Hello, Felicity. Rover spotted you before I did. Fancy a cuppa? I have a proposition for you.'

Felicity said, 'Yes, I've got a bit of shopping, but I'll call by when I've finished.'

Over coffee, Carol said, 'The boys are going to Rhyll for Easter, but Stan said it was an imposition to ask you to look after Rover again. I didn't think you'd mind. He insists on paying you, so we can all go with a clear conscience.'

Felicity accepted readily. She'd been unleashed; this is how she would make her money-making scheme work. She leaned down and whispered to Rover, now sitting on her feet. 'You really are my lucky charm. You cheered me up over Christmas, and now you've led me to a grand plan.'

Carol returned from the kitchen with a full egg box and saw her chatting to Rover. 'He can keep a secret. I talk to him all the time. I'm being cheeky, but my friend, Sal, needs her dog walked on a Tuesday when she's visiting her mother. Can you fit her in if she pays you?'

Mission accomplished, Felicity sat back and picked up her cup. She stroked the sweet, lucky dog and said, 'I'd be delighted. The money would come in handy to take the girls away.' True indeed! But not on holiday.

Both ladies spent the rest of the day smiling as they tackled their separate post-Christmas chores. Carol had Easter in Wales to look forward to, and fate gave Felicity the means to save.

As George left for work, he said, 'I'm still making up the time I took off at Christmas. I'll be working most of the weekend. No rest for the wicked.' His theatrical sigh and 'Poor me' expression didn't fool her. Her heart sank. It hadn't been a nightmare; it was reality.

Felicity's main chance of earning surreptitious funds came from her friends at the local church. The large congregation gave her access to many women for whom her newfound services would become a luxury within their means. By word of mouth, she soon became a lifeline in doggie emergencies. She could perform dog sitting, dog walking, and occasionally daytime babysitting without George knowing.

When she turned herself into a paid help, she had not imagined that her casual acquaintances at church would deepen as she became a confidante, involved in personal, hidden aspects of their lives. Her customers agreed she was a lifesaver because she helped anyone at a moment's notice. She was a good friend, not judgemental, and an occasional shoulder to cry on. Some women could not afford cash, so Felicity accepted payment in eggs, cabbages and home-baked loaves, taking the equivalent prices from her weekly housekeeping. She was always grateful for these local grocery offerings; they boosted her ready cash.

Felicity grasped other opportunities. It was amazing how many "one-off emergencies" occurred in the lives of neighbours and friends. These included houseplant watering and cat feeding while their owners were away. She squirrelled away her pennies in a tea caddy pushed to the back of the lowest shelf in the kitchen cupboard.

A machinist by trade, Felicity's escape fund also increased by taking up hems and making minor clothing alterations. The most straightforward and highest earner was when she revived favourite clothes by replacing broken zips. She was amused to discover a latent talent as a covert home-based entrepreneur.

Confidence restored, she was ready to confide in her plan and turned to Auntie Mabel, the only person who could help her.

Chapter 7

Mabel enjoyed her busy managerial post at The Wellington. Manchester's city centre was so busy, and she became popular, lending a hand or giving advice to anyone who needed it. Customers often urged her to open a bar or club, but she enjoyed the flattery; although financially out of her league, the possibility percolated from time to time.

In September 1939, the war against Germany had just begun, and a sprinkling of servicemen entered The Wellington. Most nights, young men asked if she knew somewhere cosier than the rough pub atmosphere. They wanted coffee and a quiet chat rather than beer over shouting. The concept triggered an idea for Mabel, '*If this is the market for these clients, where is the venue?*'

One sunny evening, Mabel walked the half-hour home to Ardwick Green instead of taking the tram. She needed to blow away the sickly smell of beer and tobacco clinging to her hair and clothes. At the approach to London Road Station, a glance down a narrow road revealed an intriguing *For Sale* sign. She checked her watch and nodded; only six-thirty, plenty of time. At the end of the street, cumulous clouds, tinged with peach, framed the sun as it bounced its orange rays along the brickwork, enticing her toward the empty building.

Mabel walked briskly towards the beckoning sign and discovered a disused billiards hall. Billiards had fallen out of favour, replaced by pool, which moved players to renovated pubs in the top storey of department stores.

The hall wore a sad, neglected air; as it had languished on the market for months. Underneath the grimy frontage was a handsome building flanked by small one-room shops. She rubbed the dust off a window and peered through. The interior needs renovation, knocking through both sides and fresh paint on the walls.' Then she strolled around the perimeter of the building. '*At face value, the exterior looks in reasonable nick.*'

With her imagination fired up, she pulled out a pen and paper from her handbag and scribbled down the telephone number. On the walk home, her mind raced with ideas. *'I'll build a lounge area to offer snacks and tea, besides alcohol. Those young servicemen, new to the city, from The Wellington, will be my target.'*

She tossed and turned during the night, and her mind produced a vivid picture by dawn. She sipped her morning tea. 'I must do this. My savings will be a good deposit. I'll contact the owner now while I'm brave.'

The elderly owner was enthusiastic about her idea and laughed. 'It's been standing empty, earning nothing for me. What's your best offer?'

Mabel went for it and presented a silly offer that he readily accepted. 'In good faith, I can deposit the lion's share using my savings.'

He said, 'I can be flexible about the outstanding balance of payment. If your project succeeds, I have unloaded the property. If it fails and you can't pay me, it will be easier for me to sell after you've tarted it up. No hurry for the cash, I can't lose either way.'

Mabel said, 'That suits us both. Will you get the paperwork done? I don't know where to start.'

'Of course. Leave that to me. Give me your details, and I'll be back in touch later to complete everything.'

She replaced the receiver and staggered to the hall chair with trembling legs to digest the meaningful discussion.

Two days later, she met the owner at the premises and toured the interior. The club comprised a large open hall with toilet facilities, a storeroom, and a bar along one side. There was plenty of space for her to annexe a kitchen and a personal relaxation area.

True to his word, the owner soon had the documentation executed and arranged a basic survey for her, and she kept working at The Wellington to earn money for the remodelling.

Three long-standing friends and customers offered ad hoc services. Charlie, a plumber; Bill, a builder; and Sid, a carpenter. Their expertise at the planning stage saved her the expense of an architect. They offered a few hours a week, which Mabel could afford, which quickly increased, keeping pace with their enthusiasm and shortening the renovation time. They didn't get paid immediately, but they knew she wouldn't let them down.

Sid was confident with any aspect of woodworking. Nothing fazed him; from floorboards to ceiling joists, he was adept. With Mabel, he sourced and renovated old second-hand chairs, tables, and armchairs. Bill could turn his hand to anything in the building line. Sturdy, balding with broad square fingers, calloused from handling bricks, he seemed tireless as he replaced tiles and laid carpets. Charlie was a jovial plumber with a polished red face, always happy to solder pipework.

All three workmen continued their daytime jobs, but their interests centred on the club. The men were happier being answerable to no one. Even with delayed monetary rewards, the rise in their self-worth was inestimable.

Mabel, anticipating retirement from The Wellington, was ostensibly training a new manager, which meant she could leave the pub earlier on the quiet nights in the market area.

It was only a matter of weeks before the club was ready for business. Mabel's friend Jenny, an office worker, dealt with the paperwork, learning as she went along. She contacted breweries, grocers, and bakeries and grew with and into her job at the club. Initially, she spent an hour at Mabel's new venture, which increased with variety and fun. When funds became available, Jenny got paid. Her brilliant butterfly mind flew from project to project.

One day, a large box appeared at the club with her name stencilled on the top. The workers prodded the outside, dying to know the contents. They couldn't wait for her to start work.

It took two of them to lift her prize from its wrapping. They laughed when they saw it was an ancient typewriter. Feigning hurt, she said, 'Hey, it was free from my previous office, pushed to the back of a cupboard. It still works, and I've scrounged a few scraps of paper to show you.'

'Into the office,' they cried, pointing to the corner of their makeshift lounge, which held a desk. Jenny sat in front of the black metal contraption. She proudly placed the paper on the roller and scrolled it to the right place. Her fingers jumped up and down furiously on the round letters. With a flourish, she pulled the paper out to show them, and they checked the wording. No spelling mistakes; Jenny's dexterity on the keys undoubtedly impressed the cynical bystanders.

Mabel surveyed this small disparate band of tradesmen forging ahead with their combined dreams, creating a vibrant, welcoming place for the servicemen. The club was running well, but she needed someone she trusted to relieve her from time to time. She knew who to contact and started writing an invitation letter.

Chapter 8

Two weeks previously, Mabel had received the letter from Felicity. She reread it and couldn't believe it was her niece asking for help and support to leave George, who had been leading a double life.

Sitting with the letter in her hand, she thought, *'How did I read him so wrong'.* As an agony aunt and an impartial ear to her male customers in the pubs, she became an excellent judge of character over the years. *'George seemed to me to be what is called a billboard of a figure; has no apparent depths.'*

Although Mabel had known him for years, she still felt ill at ease when alone with him. Her attempts at chatting bounced off the wall of his indifference and made her remarks sound banal. He never lowered his newspaper to talk, so she usually picked up any handy item or returned a cup to the kitchen to escape.

She had seen him chatting and laughing with other people, so he wasn't always taciturn. Felicity told her he was an uninspiring parent but a good husband and generous. Mabel had no qualms about leaving Felicity with him when she moved to Manchester.

Mabel posted the invitation letter to Felicity asking her to come and join forces. Mabel's wages from managing The Wellington would be ample to cover their living expenses until they had earnings from the club.

Felicity wrote back immediately to Mabel.

"...I'm ready to come to Manchester and want to bring the girls. I've been working on an escape fund and gathered a tidy amount. It's fired me up to concentrate on something positive. Please send me more details and when I should go over it with you. The girls know nothing of George's infidelity and I dread telling them. Perhaps we can discuss it when we meet up? ...'

With the positive response, Mabel could now slot her niece and her savings into the club plans. She continued to work at the pub and soon completed the club renovations.

Mabel's reply came two days later, suggesting they meet the following Saturday.

"... *Bring your cash, and we'll go to the Post Office and open an account. When we tell the girls about George, I'd be thrilled if they want to join us, but really it's up to them where and how they wish to continue their lives...*"

Felicity told George she was taking the girls to Manchester on Saturday to do some shopping and would stay overnight with Auntie Mabel. He shrugged, disguising his pleasure. He could now see Polly this weekend without time constraints and may even ask to stay overnight with her.

Mabel was waiting to greet them at the station. She was delighted to see Anna and Betsy and how grown up they were. After an afternoon mooching around the department stores, they enjoyed catching up over a noisy dinner at home.

Near the end, during a lull, Felicity started the sad story she'd rehearsed. 'I don't know how to start, but your father's been keeping another family in Nantwich. They have a girl and a boy.'

Anna shouted, 'Bloody hell. She's right. I told Mum I saw them just before Christmas in Lewis's.'

'Sorry, Anna. It was a shock, so I covered for George until I knew more.'

Betsy couldn't believe what she was hearing, and her head ping-ponged between Anna and her mother as the story unfolded.

Felicity, stony-faced, resumed the tale. 'Yes, Betsy. It's true. She saw them together, but I had to confirm it. So, over the months, I've been earning cash for us from my various part-time jobs. I feel quite insecure, and if your father continues to share us, I can't live with his lies. We'd be really stuck if he abandons us to live with his other family.'

'So, he's still seeing them?' Betsy asked.

Felicity hated seeing her stricken face, 'I'm sorry, but yes. George still doesn't know that I found out. I bet if we returned earlier, there'd be no-one at home.'

Anna pursed her lips and wriggled in her chair. 'So you've sat on his deceit all this time. What now?'

Felicity looked at Mabel, 'Dear Auntie Mabel here, has kindly offered us the spare rooms in this house if you wish to move.'

Mabel nodded and spoke softly, 'That's right. Your mum and I have a plan. An old billiards hall became available to convert into a club for servicemen on leave. I bought it, and I'm renovating it. My wages are good at the pub, so I'll continue to work there. It will keep us going during the club's start-up.'

Intrigued, Anna asked, 'Where do we fit in?'

'Well, I hope you, Felicity and Betsy, can come here full-time. There's a job as a machinist with a friend of mine. His firm is expanding to manufacture tents, rucksacks, and heavy goods for the army. It has brilliant prospects for the future.'

The girls looked at each other, riveted to their seats in disbelief.

Mabel calmly said, 'Don't say anything just yet, but talk it over carefully with your mum.'

Anna said, 'How could he? I can't believe it - Mum's blameless. No wonder we hardly saw him.'

Betsy nodded and gave her two pennyworths. 'Dad never was a bundle of laughs.'

Over the girls' heads, the two older women exchanged glances of relief. Felicity thought, *'Young people can be surprising. They've dismissed their father as a rotter who was never that close to them. In their eyes, he's become a shadowy figure by his long absences.'*

An animated chat ensued about their futures. Indignation at the treatment of their mother took over, and Anna said, 'We'll show him. He'll not mess us about. Besides, I'd like to move to the city; there's lots more going on. My job's quite boring, and I'd like to find a better class of boyfriend.'

Betsy laughed, knowing to whom Anna was referring. 'When can we move in?' she asked, fuelled by Anna's positivity.

Felicity almost wept; they viewed the upheaval as an adventure, not a disaster. She said, 'It'll take time, and I'm afraid you'll have to be involved in the deception. We'll keep a few clothes in each place to avoid your father finding out about our move before we're ready. I want to avoid any unpleasant scenes. We'll leave when everything is in place; it will be quick, without drama.'

Anna added with bitterness, 'He wouldn't notice. He's never there.'

Felicity added that they would have fun scouring the junk shops to replace their few treasured pictures and minor furniture items. They would then feel at home with familiar objects around them when they eventually transferred to Mabel's house.

Little did they know, but Felicity's decisive, meaningful lifestyle change would be pivotal in all four lives.

Chapter 9

The public felt no immediate impact after the dramatic announcement by Prime Minister Neville Chamberlain at 11.15 a.m. on Sunday, 3 September 1939. On The Home Service he announced that "This country is at war with Germany.'

To avoid the expected bombing, two schools on the outskirts of Crewe had taken in children evacuated from the centre of Manchester. When nothing happened, the evacuee children trickled back home. Unprepared for conflict, an arms race developed. This lull was known as the "Phoney War".

The Authorities advised George he would not be called up as he worked in essential engineering, in what they considered a "safe job". Keeping personnel and supplies moving was paramount.

Two months later, Mabel hastily wrote to Felicity,

"...If you're still serious about joining me, now would be the right time. I'll keep my job as the pub manageress as I expect no income from the club yet and I want you to be a permanent presence and hands-on help. Payment from your fund towards rental and household bills would ease the immediate cash situation. The war effort's gathering pace, and we must take this opportunity and open the club..."

"Give me a week!" Felicity wrote back. Her excitement was tinged with fear. It was a massive step for anyone to take, let alone a suburban housewife with two teenage children.

Mabel received the letter with glee; all her longed-for wishes were happening in one stroke. Her three dearest people were coming to live with her. She busied herself at home, creating enough space for them.

Felicity told her close friends about her impending departure and gave them the impression it was a temporary move to help her auntie set up a project for a war effort assisting service members. She returned her books to the library with a casual farewell and thanked Miss Smith, the librarian.

She wanted nothing from the house of monetary value, only sentimental keepsakes. She wondered wryly, *'I wonder if he pays more attention to any items in his other home? I'll leave him to deal with the milk, coal and newspapers.'*

Intense hurt and resentment swept through her again. She occasionally wept in private but afterwards felt stronger, fierce and robust, knowing she acted in her own best interests and that of her girls'.

The leaving day arrived. Felicity feigned sleep until George left for work. She felt elated but terrified as she prepared to jump into the unknown abyss ahead. *'Today's the day we join Mabel, leaving this home and George behind. I've tried to plan every detail, like a general prepared to do a major battle.'*

Anna's tousled red mop of hair appeared around the door. 'Morning Mum, I've made tea and toast downstairs. We'll get dressed later.'

Betsy was already tucking into her breakfast when Felicity came down. 'Alright, girls. Are you sure you want to go through with this?'

They replied with a resounding, 'Yes!'

The most significant step was when they brought out fully packed cases from their hiding places and stacked them in the hall, an omen of irrevocable movement.

Their deadline was nine o'clock when the hired car would take them to the station. Felicity had booked it a week ago at the newsagent, who lifted his eyebrows at someone requesting a vehicle for a destination of such a short walk away. She stood firm and didn't explain.

The women stood in the hall. Felicity inwardly prayed, *'Please let the car be on time. I couldn't bear it if something stopped us from going now. Just let us get on our way.'*

Five minutes later, the driver had stowed the copious amount of luggage in the boot.

The girls stood at the car, astounded by the finality of their actions. They watched their mother put the large key in the door. She took one last look at the four-leaf clover key fob and superstitiously thought that she might be throwing away her luck. Conscious of the waiting car, she dismissed this idea and, without hesitation, turned the key with a quick flick as if it would detonate, pulled it out and pushed it hard through the letterbox. She ran the few steps to the car, and silently the girls bundled into the back seat while Felicity pulled a weak smile as she sat next to the driver.

He initially thought his passengers were going on holiday, but when he saw their stark white faces and no bubbly girly conversation, he just set off without his usual banter.

The girls sat in the back, and Anna leaned forward, ready to wave if she saw anyone she knew, as people usually hired cars for weddings and funerals. Betsy rested her hand on her mother's shoulder, suddenly needing physical contact.

At the station, the driver left them in the car while he brought a porter's trolley and loaded the cases. He led the way as the women trailed behind. He opened the carriage door and lifted the luggage in.

Felicity suddenly opened her handbag to retrieve the money for a tip. He covered her hand, 'No need. Short journey. Good luck.'

She nodded and swallowed to remove the lump in her throat.

They watched him leave the platform, and Betsy broke the peace, 'Wasn't he kind?'

The train doors slammed one after the other, a whistle blew, and Felicity could finally relax. *'Thank God. I've done it. The past has passed, so what's the future?'*

Seeing Mabel on the Manchester platform was a tremendous relief. After quick hugs between the women, they hurried after the porter to the taxi.

At Mabel's house, the girls ran two stairs at a time up to their room, eager to be reacquainted with their treasures installed over the previous weeks. While in the kitchen, Felicity staggered over to Mabel, arms outstretched, pressed her face onto her aunt's chest and finally wept copiously with relief.

To comfort her, Mabel whispered, 'It is a hugely brave thing you have done. Leaving your home was probably the hardest part, and you've done it. You'll see, everything will be alright here. Welcome to your new home.'

Many miles away, George was sure Felicity hadn't noticed his long absences during the past few months. All seemed to function normally at home, with the girls, so it was a surprise late that evening when his usual, 'I'm home!' got no reply. As he stepped towards the kitchen, he noticed the door had pushed something towards the wall. As he stooped to pick it up, he recognised the fob from Felicity's door key. '*She must have dropped it.*'

Chapter 10

George strolled into the kitchen, checking for any food left out for him. Mystified, he picked up a sealed envelope on the kitchen table addressed to him. He opened it with trepidation.

"Dear George,

I have taken the girls with me to live with Auntie Mabel in Manchester. There's plenty of work there for us.

My feelings are not strong enough to share you with your other family. It was before Christmas when we found out about your affair. I've not discussed this with you to spare any distressing scenes and recriminations.

I'm serious about my intention to start a new life with more opportunities; please don't try to contact us.'

Felicity."

He stared ahead and held onto the kitchen table, and his stomach tightened as he reread the brief note. The careful writing and severe wording exposed that this was not a spur-of-the-moment decision. She had known for months and planned everything. For confirmation, he bounded upstairs, and a quick check of the girls' empty bedroom and sparse wardrobe contents confirmed their actions.

He said out loud, 'Oh God. How could I have been so stupid?' His first taste of genuine passion had claimed his sanity. He now felt like a naughty child whose lies and misdemeanours had been rumbled. He shuffled back into the kitchen and opened a bottle of beer. The larder had bread and cheese, so he made a sandwich. Shocked and exhausted, he fell into a cold empty bed.

He woke to the realisation of his foolishness. The house was always quiet at breakfast time, but it was strange not being mindful of making a noise. He stuffed the note into his coat pocket and left for work. The day dragged, and he had trouble concentrating on putting together even simple engine parts. Lost in his thoughts, he didn't want to talk to his colleagues and kept any conversation to a minimum. He couldn't wait until five, when he would catch the train to Polly. *'Women deal better with emotional things. She'll know what to do.'*

Polly gasped when she saw George on a Monday evening, standing on her doorstep with a haggard, hunted look.

'I need to talk urgently with you,' he said. The glumness on his face and slumped shoulders alerted something was awry.

'Come in,' she offered, automatically fluffing up her hair as they entered the living room. The children splayed out on the floor, playing with toys. They looked up, thrilled to see 'Uncle George'.

After acknowledging their playtime, he stood by the fireplace for a couple of minutes. Polly didn't take long putting them to bed. On her return, he was holding out the envelope.

'What's this?' she asked as she opened it. She didn't like surprises, and this didn't feel like a good one.

'Felicity's left me and taken the girls.'

Polly's mouth drooped. Thoughts rapidly tumbled over each other. *'Should I be happy about this? Has our fling got out of hand? Do I actually want to end up with him?'* She skimmed the note, immediately decided what she wanted and looked straight at him unyieldingly.

It stunned George how distant she had become in just a few seconds. Where was the shy, clinging ingenue that charmed and made him feel like a handsome hero?

She handed back the note and envelope. Her voice was icy cold. 'Go home, George and sort out your affairs. See your mother and maybe come back on Friday.'

He didn't know what he expected from Polly, perhaps some compassion. He nodded and took a step towards her to give her a parting kiss, and she stepped back.

Spurned, he smiled pathetically at her and left for home.

All week, he felt numb and went through the motions of eating, working, and staying home with a stiff upper lip. He tentatively knocked on Polly's door at seven on Friday.

She ushered him into the living room, pointing to the chair by the fire. She sat upright opposite. George took her curt stance to be a negative start to their conversation. He foolishly thought she might have thawed.

The protective mother defending her young had her speech prepared and rehearsed. 'We were both having a little fun because you were married and bored. I never wanted to become a home wrecker. My husband's family in London offered us a home, but I wanted to be here and independent. This situation has clarified things. It's time to settle my children in permanent schooling, so we'll return to London next week. I'm sorry this has happened to you, but it's not really my problem.'

It felt futile to respond. Polly had decided her future was not with him, so he nodded and left dejected. He sat in a daze on the crowded, smoky Crewe train. Felicity's sudden leaving had severed his dalliance. He pondered his next step. *'I've lost the most meaningful women in my life in one stroke. I've coasted along on life's road, smoothed by powerful females. It leaves only one more dominant woman to see - my mother.'*

Chapter 11

Without his family, the house was eerily tranquil for a Saturday. After George had finished the few household chores, he was tempted to have a beer for courage but opted for strong tea; he couldn't risk alcohol on his breath when he faced his mother that afternoon. But face her, he must, plus any criticism or ridicule from friends and neighbours.

He felt for Felicity's note in his coat pocket and lifted the polished knocker on the shiny painted front door. He needed to tell his mother before word got around. She was an upright, sometimes sanctimonious, true pillar of her Christian faith.

'George! Whatever is the matter?' noting the misery on his chalk-white face.

He blurted out, 'Felicity's left me, taken the girls to Manchester to Auntie Mabel's.' He held out the crumpled letter and shook with vigorous, manly grief.

She never embraced people but managed an arm and a few strong pats across his heaving shoulder. She took the note, held his elbow, and steered him into the parlour. He sat at the polished table, his head in his hands.

She read the letter and looked over her glasses at him, 'We'll sort this out.' She wanted to believe the best of her beloved son, who, in her eyes, had obviously been led astray. It was her duty to support him.

As she busied herself with tea and cake, always necessary in a crisis, she asked, 'Was this one brief affair? Is it over?'

He nodded. 'Polly and her kids will return to her family in London.'

'Well, that's that then. Felicity's been scorned and made a strong, calculated point. It might be some time before she returns.' Ethel spent no time and seized the opportunity to bring her son into the fold. Her lodgers had recently moved out, and she felt lonely and

47

missed the extra money it brought in. Having her son as a replacement for both was a timely Godsend.

'George, there is no point in paying rent for your empty house. Move in with me until it's smoothed over.' Her injured son needed her; a maternal instinct stopped her from making a pertinent religious speech. 'Everyone can make one mistake. I'm sure, in time, Felicity will forgive you.'

It amazed him that his mother had already suggested a quick and constructive way out of his massive problem. He saw what she was doing; she wanted to appease her loneliness and feel wanted again. On his side, he dreaded going back to an empty house. He hated cooking; financially, this could be the most sensible short-term solution for both of them.

Ethel said, 'We will go to your church tomorrow. If necessary, we can explain that Felicity's leaving is a temporary separation. It's the truth and not unusual.'

He felt his mother's claws already pinching him, pulling him into her lair. But the next day, when he stood next to her as they assembled outside the church in the chilly air, he watched his magnificent mother getting ready to manage the enquirers.

To their surprise, there was no ridicule or criticism, only one remark from a congregation member. 'How kind of Felicity to go help her relative. Setting up a new enterprise as part of the war effort is admirable. You'll be going to see her on weekends, I expect?'

George forced a smile through the charade. The sensible next move was for him to give notice on the rented house, transfer most of his clothes to his mother's, and pack the rest of his family life into cardboard boxes. Chastened, he buckled down to work and enjoyed a few quiet evenings at the Railway Worker's Club each week. His mother fussed over him so much that he didn't miss Felicity and the girls.

He was intrigued, though; the facing-saving details Felicity gave her church friends could signal a plausible way to cover her back, no matter the outcome.

His fatal mistake had been underestimating his wife; since they had met, she had strengthened and gleaned an education, but he hadn't taken much notice. The meticulous planning over months was not the action of a weak, forgiving spouse. She left no space for explanation or recriminations.

His mother interrupted his gloomy pondering, reading aloud from the local press.

'How interesting! The first evacuees from Birmingham and Manchester have arrived in Crewe, suggesting the inevitable bombardment of the major cities. War creates a melting pot for so many lives. Perhaps your family will return to the comparative safety of Crewe sooner than any of us thought.'

He nodded in agreement. *'Felicity might not have won after all.'*

Chapter 12

The Navy, Army and Air Force Institutes (NAAFI) canteens were functional and stark, so Mabel's idea in 1939 of providing a homely venue for servicemen was original. Jenny contacted the welfare departments of the armed services to sound out Mabel's plan, which they welcomed and encouraged.

In no time, the club became a fount of knowledge and held addresses of respectable boarding houses, inns, and local amenities. Jenny gathered information on transport, buses, and train schedules. She became invaluable and worked hard performing simple office duties until she had learned enough to become an executive, a novelty in a world where few women flourished at that level.

No fanfare of trumpets sounded at the official opening of the club. They were still adding the finishing touches when the first trickle of customers arrived. The servicemen wanted information, a cup of tea, and to read the newspapers. Some returned for a pint in the evening if they stayed locally. Some were young, and it was the first time they'd been away from home. Mabel gave them confidence with her motherly presence. Her curly steely grey hair and brown eyes added an air of capability. These were lads on short leave, where it was impractical to return to their distant homes.

The recruits came for the bright lights, but naïve and alone, they were unsure where to start. So, they usually settled down to a pleasant evening, playing darts and chatting. In passing, they made easy friendships, and for many, it became a home from home, and they forgot about living it up in the city as they became entangled in the safety net of Mabel's club.

The young males who frequented their club intrigued Felicity. She hadn't had much contact with men. Her father was in the army for four years, which traumatised him so much that he became introverted, just a shell of himself with no appetite or energy for banter.

Anna had a job lined up, which comprised training on heavier sewing machines and making goods like tents and canvas rucksacks. This was better than sewing garments, the best specialist tuition she could ever receive. The factory owner, Mr Timpson, saw a practical and dexterous girl eager to earn a living and learn a trade. She was already a part-time machinist and helped in the club with her mother when required.

Felicity turned her hand to renovating the junk shop finds and oddments Mabel had bought in sales. With Sid, they painted the chairs white and recovered the easy chairs with matching textured material in shades of yellow. It was bright, modern, and inviting to its young customers. A large room with lofty ceilings and windows set high on the solid walls gave a feeling of permanence and strength. They had left the brick walls plastered and painted white, providing a suitable background texture.

When it was up and running, Mabel gathered the other founders, Felicity, Jenny, Bill, Sid and Charlie, to celebrate. They congratulated themselves on their spectacular achievement, which had changed them all as they unearthed hidden gifts and strengths.

Mabel paid off the three men with some of Felicity's escape funds. This cash enabled them to buy equipment, and instilled confidence to start their own businesses, usually something that needed second-hand ladders and an old van.

One evening, Mabel and Felicity leaned, elbows on the counter, and gazed at the youths, not big drinkers, enjoying themselves engrossed in darts, playing cards and chatting, a retreat from regimentation. Many had been away from home for long stretches. After the first heady taste of freedom from parental restrictions, they expected excitement but were homesick. They missed their unique bonds with siblings and even shared dogeared photos of their beloved pets. In the club, barriers between the various armed services disappeared as they founded new alliances.

Felicity and Mabel co-managed the club, but only one needed to be on duty during the quiet times. Their luxury item was a cleaner who rushed around every day before opening. To avoid unwanted attention in this den of masculinity, they practised deceit and "put it about" that Felicity wasn't sexually interested in men. A face devoid of make-up, hair scraped back, and dark overalls created a low profile. Her no-nonsense appearance and demeanour were convincing and not worth a second look for predators.

Privileged to play a part in the war effort, Mabel looked thoughtful. 'Have you noticed our lads are mainly army and navy, so we can safely refer to ourselves as an "army and navy" club?

In the early war days, the lads took many trips to the air-raid shelter, but Mabel never left the club, like a captain staying with her ship. Bombs rained down on Manchester, with munitions factories as their prime targets.

Felicity said, 'The raids are not so frequent now. I hope those sirens won't start up too soon.' As they surveyed the bar area, the urgent wail of the warning siren broke the peaceful silence.

She laughed, 'Speak of the devil. Off we go,' and hung her rough apron up behind the bar and marshalled her young charges, persuading them to follow her into the nearby shelter, a cellar stacked with benches and stools. The air filled with the acrid smell of the kerosene lamps as the motley groups made themselves comfortable. Being a city centre with offices and shops, few children appeared; most workers stopped their activities, if practical, and trooped to the air-raid shelter.

Felicity thought how ironic it was that she fled to an open cultural city just as it became restricted by war. She had envisaged a smart city life but had entered something entirely different. The lights dimmed with the ululating sounds of the sirens, and spotters relayed aerial progress as the waves of enemy bombers swept overhead under cover of darkness.

She snuggled into her cosy woollen blanket and looked around at the grimy walls. They faded into insignificance as colourful characters hurried in, swathed in vivid blankets and old patchwork eiderdowns, carrying flasks of hot drinks. Housewives stepped into the vacant jobs of the soldiers on the front line. Overnight, women removed their make-up and rolled their hair in curlers, ready for work the following day.

Some pencilled love letters through suppressed tears for men who may not return. The sirens and grim surroundings were potent symbols of being under attack. There was no front line or boundary in this worldwide war.

A few teenage boys bustled into the shelter and joked as they opened their guitar cases. Their previous patrons in the pub ignored their amateurish musical offerings. It was a lucky night for musicians, as an appreciative captive audience was hungry for diversion from the bombardment above.

When the music started, the tired grey faces transformed into bright smiles as if a make-believe magic wand wafted over them. Defiantly, they shook their clenched fists into the air and sang as loud as possible, reverberating around the cellar walls. Their spirits lifted; they slept in the chairs and benches. Some leaned together, propping each other up, or the weary heads rested on the laps of their loved ones.

The all-clear's insistent, high-pitched, level tone was always welcome. The sun rose as the shelterers presumed they were safe and stiffly shuffled out into the frosty dawn air.

The raids usually started when Mabel and Felicity were still in the club; it was foolhardy to return to the girls in Ardwick Green. Anna and Betsy were sensible teenagers; when the sirens sounded, they automatically reached for their capacious carryalls, loaded with blow-up pillows, old eiderdowns, thick socks, notebooks, pencils and magazines. They carried another satchel with rent books, birth certificates and precious photographs in case their house got bombed. The girls quickly made a vacuum flask of hot cocoa and grabbed a packet of biscuits.

Dressed in heavy clothes and boots, they locked up and crossed the main road clearing and joined people coming for refuge from all directions to the deep warehouse cellars, one of the many designated air-raid shelters scattered over the city.

The council had done their best to make these cellars habitable, even cosy. They white-washed the rough bricks, mounted electric lights, and arranged assorted wooden seating and benches in circles. When the time came, the authorities dimmed the lights, signalling to doss down and try to rest.

Groups of friends and workmates nervously chatted together and tried to ignore the cacophony of crashing and thumping from the bombs and falling masonry. Others were not so lucky to be near a shelter and sought refuge under arches next to the railway station, sharing the space with horses, wagons and delivery vans.

All over the cities, thousands survived the Blitz by burrowing in cellars below the tall buildings, like wild animals seeking safety in their lairs.

Mabel arranged easy chairs to make beds for the hardened and blasé who remained in the club. Strong, fragrant coffee bubbled and welcomed the shelterers' return.

Chapter 13

Emma, Felicity's friend from Crewe, visited to exchange news. But just before she left, Emma said, 'It's filtered through that George is living full-time with his mother.

Felicity was perplexed, 'What happened to the girlfriend?'

'She was actually a widow and he didn't move in with her. As soon as she found out you'd gone, she hot-footed it back to London with her children. Apparently, it had just been a fun diversion for her. The children weren't even his.'

Felicity's face turned white as she took in this new information. 'Widow? Those children aren't his. Are you sure?'

Emma nodded. 'Quite sure. The affair didn't even last the year.'

'Oh my God, what have I done?' Felicity thought.

Emma continued gaily. 'I never believed that George was devious enough to carry on a double life. He even got caught out by his own daughter.' She laughed, looked at her watch, and then noticed the shocked face of her friend.

'Are you OK? I'm sorry, I thought you knew. Well, it's better the news should come from me than anyone else,' she said as she left, 'I'll visit again soon.'

Felicity no longer resented George. She had gradually experienced a sea change, but some things still baffled her, *'Why did he do it, and what was lacking in me?'*

An hour later, Mabel came in from the club. 'Betsy's holding the fort. It's so quiet there you have time to have your meal before you go.' Her voice trailed off as she caught sight of her niece slumped in the chair with a bleak expression.

Felicity repeated Emma's bombshell. 'I feel so selfish and guilty now. Why didn't I challenge him at the time? Anna and I jumped to the same conclusion before we established the facts. I know now that I secretly grabbed it as my only chance and a great excuse to move out of a loveless and dull marriage.'

Mabel said, 'I never really thought they were his children. Well, I, for one, am so pleased that you came here. It's been a lot of fun, and the girls have really fitted in. We have a lovely life together.'

Felicity looked forlorn, 'But I made them think he's a real rotter who mistreated all of us. I must admit my mistake and tell them I was also at fault.'

Mabel put on her coat. 'Don't be too hard on yourself. You're not the one who had an affair. Listen, I've eaten. Why don't you stay here and have dinner and a conversation with the girls? I'll go and close the club early. Anna's due home soon, so I'll send Betsy along too.'

Felicity was grateful to Mabel for stepping in. She hadn't been looking forward to spending the evening trying to be friendly to their young patrons at the club.

Over the unusually quiet family dinner, the girls looked at each other, and Anna raised her eyebrows at Betsy. *Could their mother have something profound to say?* Felicity had said very little and seemed distracted. Mabel returned from the club and joined the excruciating silence around the table. Everyone concentrated on Felicity and waited for her to speak.

With a croaky voice, she said, 'I heard today that your father had not been living a double life. Those two children weren't his. The lady cut the affair short when she heard that we'd left. It was George's only lapse in all our married years and I should have confronted him. He never had a chance to explain.'

She stared at the table, unable to face her daughters' reactions, and continued, 'Anna and I jumped to the wrong conclusion. It was a short fling; he probably never intended to leave us. It seems the widow didn't want him long-term, and it was just a bit of summer fun for them. She soon scuttled back to her family in London, and George moved in with his mother.'

Anna, frank and uncomplicated, twisted a strand of red hair and said, 'Mum, there is only one thing for you to consider. Do you want to go back to him and your old life?'

Betsy looked agitated, so Felicity dabbed at her watery eyes and broke in quickly. 'Plenty for us to think about, but there's no hurry. I just wanted you to know the truth about your father. He was never a monster, just foolish, and we should forgive him. Everyone makes mistakes.'

Anna glanced at Betsy, who nodded on seeing her big sister accept the situation.

'To answer your question, Anna, I do not want to go back. At almost forty, I'm enjoying my independence. However, this new information has led us to a crossroads. Knowing the truth, you may think differently of him and me. I selfishly pulled you away from your father, friends and lifestyle. You're not just mine, also his daughters, and must have time to consider the rest of your lives. You might prefer to return to Crewe to be nearer him and your grandmother.'

Felicity walked into the kitchen, straightened her back, took a deep breath and suddenly felt a load lifted from her mind. The girls' bewildered faces lit up when she returned confidently with a tray laden with tea. Just what they all needed to lighten the situation.

She said, 'I've been thinking. The separation must have really hurt your grandmother. None of it was her fault. She's always been kind and helpful. I'd like it if you could find it in you to contact her and your father. We sometimes make bad judgements in our relationships; we must repair them if we can and move on.'

Betsy finally found her voice, 'There are always some casualties when an affair occurs.'

Felicity smiled at these wise words coming from her youngest. 'Girls, I made another grave miscalculation. I didn't realise the major cities would take the force of the Blitzkrieg. I unwittingly put both of you in danger, bringing you here when you would have been safer in Crewe.'

Mabel cut in to defend her. 'No one knew where and what would be blitzed. In hindsight, as a family, look at what a substantial contribution we made to the war effort and under bombardment! Anna made equipment for the army, Betsy sewed uniforms, and we provided a modest haven for the boys on leave. Still around us are swathes of the city, still full of rubble. So we were, in our own way, at the front, helping our soldiers where we could.'

They lapsed into a stunned silence at Mabel's unusual outburst. They were so preoccupied with their own affairs; they didn't realise it until now, but any action they chose would be life-changing for her, too.

Felicity said, 'Let's all take a week to think seriously about what action would make us happy and the ramifications for each of us.'

The subject swirled around the household for the week without a mention. Everyone needed to come up with a heartfelt answer to, "Go back or stay".

Chapter 14

The following Sunday, the club opened only during the day, giving the family time to be together during the evening. After an early dinner, Mabel poured herself a light ale and slowly sank into an easy chair. *'This is the day of reckoning. What the girls decide will happen next could change everything.'*

With everyone seated, she couldn't wait any longer. 'Well?' she asked and stared at them one by one, memorising their faces. The floodgates opened; everyone spoke at once. Anna stood up, eager to make her well-practised speech. She looked straight at Mabel.

'Betsy and I want to stay here with Mum and you. Dad was always working, rarely at home; he was little more than a stranger when we left, so we never really missed him. Mum, you told him not to bother us, so perhaps we should contact him and grandma; now we know the truth.'

With her speech over, Anna sat down and relaxed. Betsy looked at her big sister with admiration and nodded vigorously, trying not to applaud. They had acknowledged the importance of the situation.

Mabel gulped and tried to stop herself from weeping in delight. She felt for the handkerchief neatly folded in her sleeve, just in case.

Felicity stood, gave the assembled women a crooked smile, and hurried towards the kitchen. 'Well, that's settled then. I'll make the tea.' She filled the kettle, grabbed the nearest tea towel and wiped her eyes.

Intense emotion charged the room. Everyone wanted to shout, laugh or cry but just sat composed, and the tension slowly drained as they sipped their drinks.

Felicity thought, *'Nothing has actually happened, but mentally everything's changed. It forced us to pause, examine our priorities and our place.'* She smiled, *'I'd never considered myself a wronged woman.'* Her life and future were again in her own hands.

Anna marched into the hallway, took a deep breath, unhooked the phone and dialled. Betsy stood next to her as her sister spoke. 'Hello, Dad, it's Anna.'

George was taken aback, 'Anna! Has something happened? Is anything wrong with Betsy?'

'Oh no. We're all well. She's here with me now. I'm calling because we want to see you and Grandma and put the past behind us.' She waited, and her hands started shaking, wondering what he would say. She looked at Betsy for strength.

Anna heard him call out. 'Mum. It's Anna. The girls want to visit us. Is that alright?'

She heard her muffled Grandma's voice. 'Marvellous. Can they come for Sunday lunch next week?'

George repeated into the phone, 'Sunday lunch next week suit you?'

Anna frowned at Betsy, whose eyes were misting over and her face started to crumple. She covered the receiver and whispered, 'Don't you dare start crying and set me off.'

She then put on a happy voice, 'Yes, Dad, We'll get the train that arrives about noon. Love to you and Grandma.'

Betsy turned, opened the door and found Felicity had been eavesdropping. There was no stemming the group tears now. Their suppressed sense of loss had been aired and brushed aside with one sweep. All it took was one positive step.

George looked at his mother, who was blowing her nose in her pinny and thought, 'This is the first time I've actually seen her overcome with joy.' Reverting to their normal stolid conversation, he steadied his voice and said, 'After their visit, you can go to the evening service for a change. Why don't we have roast beef to celebrate?'

Ethel beamed at him allowing her happiness to shine out. She inwardly prayed at this good news, *'Thanks be to God.'*

Chapter 15

One afternoon in the autumn of 1943, Mabel polished the glasses in the club and stacked the coffee mugs behind the bar. She enjoyed this quiet part, preparing for the busy evening ahead. The number of customers had steadily increased over the few years she'd been running it.

A shadow from the door blocked the light, and a soft Californian voice interrupted Mabel's daydreaming, and she looked up. 'Hi! Ma-am. I think you can help me. I hear you hold lists of local hotels and transport.'

The strange voice came from an older American serviceman dressed in an impeccably tailored beige uniform with a polished leather belt. He was so attractive; she thought he must be a film star, with his short thick black hair, dark brown eyes, and light tan. His smile showed perfect teeth, of course.

'Yes, the brochures are over there,' said Mabel and pointed to a side table. She noted every detail of this unusual visitor.

He picked a couple out of the pile. 'Thanks. I'll be staying around this area for a week.'

She covered her amazement by pulling out a comfortable chair for him. 'Real coffee?' she asked as he looked like the type who wouldn't touch a bottled one.

'Sure. Nice.' He settled his tall, athletic frame into an armchair. He looked around at the bright modern furnishings highlighted in the slanting sunlight.

Mabel tried to make polite conversation. 'Am I allowed to ask where you're stationed?'

'Yeah, it ain't hush-hush. Warrington. I heard Manchester was an ideal base to spend my leave, plenty to explore.' He sniffed the coffee's aroma and then sipped it. 'This is an interesting place. Was it a church or a school?'

'It was a billiards hall originally. We've done it up for servicemen.' Mabel said. 'What are you planning to do here?'

'I hope to retrace the route made by my parents from Italy to America.'

Impressed, Mabel assured him staying in the city centre was an excellent idea. Transport was frequent and reliable and fanned out to all the suburbs. 'In a week, you can cover most places of interest. Have you got somewhere to stay?'

'I was hoping you could help me out there. Big hotels with identical stark rooms don't appeal to me. I fancied somewhere cosy and home-like, if possible, with local interest. The army base has hundreds of personnel, and the canteen is boringly functional, not welcoming at all.'

Mabel sifted through the brochures on the side table. 'These two pubs have rooms and might be what you're looking for. One is near the market, colourful and lively but quiet at night. The other is near the shops and restaurants. Please look at both before you decide; they are within easy walking distance of here. Either would make an excellent base for sightseeing; take my card, and they'll look after you.'

She added, 'Please come in anytime you need help or a drink. We've always got decent coffee, none of that liquid stuff.' She laughed and moved her chair a few inches closer, encouraging him to sit and finish his drink.

Felicity marched into the club to see if Mabel needed her, saw the couple poring over brochures, and sidled up to them. She pointed out the rail list and said, 'You'll save a lot of money if you travel in off-peak times.' She moved behind the bar, busied herself cleaning glasses, and couldn't help but steal a few glances at such a handsome man.

As he got up to leave, Felicity picked up an ashtray and pointed to a book on the counter. 'Would you mind signing our visitor's book, please?'

'Sure, Honey.' He signed a page with a flourish and made a few notes. He waved goodbye with his leaflets and strode outside, not carrying a kit bag but a small hold-all.

Mabel and Felicity, wide-eyed, stared at each other. Mabel said, 'It's rare to see Americans. To have an older G.I. visitor is even more unusual. Their canteens are far superior to British ones. They sell rationed stuff we just can't get.'

'Why do you call them G.I.'s?'

'It stands for government issue or general issue, something like that. It's said that G.I. stamped on American military dustbins and buckets ensured they wouldn't be sold on.'

They giggled together like schoolgirls. Felicity said, 'He looks like Clark Gable. His black eyes peer into your soul to promise tempting earthly delights!'

Mabel looked amazed at her niece's flowery language. 'What?'

Felicity murmured, 'I read it somewhere, in a romance book. It just felt appropriate,' and busied herself pretending no genuine interest in him. However, she couldn't deny he had a captivating cleft chin.

She playfully poked her aunt. 'Take your beady eyes off him; he's far too young for you.'

'Wow!' they chorused, dashed to the open doorway, and watched him slink across the road like a black panther.

Mabel said, 'Isn't he gorgeous, and with that drawl?' She sighed and reached for the visitor's book. She read out loud, 'Lieutenant Bruno Ponti. Age 40 from California. American Medical Corps. I wonder if we'll see him again?'

'I should think so. He looked very comfortable sitting there, guzzling your coffee. I can't stand those Yanks with their fancy uniforms, and what's more, I've had enough of men, for now, thank you.'

Mabel thought, *'Gosh! You're touchy'* and hurried away to serve their first evening customer.

Felicity felt prejudiced against any G.I. who offered impoverished teenage girls gifts unobtainable in the shops, mainly lipsticks, nylons, and cigarettes. They swaggered around and were often lowly farm boys masquerading as conquering heroes. The British boys wore the rough khaki uniform of army soldiers or, more informal, dark blue for the Navy. In contrast, the Americans, dressed in fine smooth beige cloth and tan leather belts, looked like officers to the average person, regardless of rank.

At seven the following evening, they were surprised to see the American again. He looked very different, with a casual navy sweater and grey pants covered by a camel trench coat. In civvies, he now blended in well. He was eager to speak with Mabel.

'I picked The Regent, but I didn't stay for coffee. I came up here instead. The manager sends you his regards.'

Mabel said, 'You chose the best one.' They chatted for a few minutes until she walked into the office. Bruno queued at the bar for a drink and watched the plain Felicity serving and making small talk with the customers. Mabel mentioned something about her niece working here, and this must be her.

The sailor seated next to him said with a knowing wink, 'Don't look at her, mate; she doesn't date men.' That intrigued Bruno; he studied her closely; blonde hair pulled back with a rubber band, not a scrap of makeup and are those grey eyes? She had bundled her slim body in an unshapely, oversized blue overall and wore flat black shoes. The other lads accepted her act, but he saw straight through it. *'What have you got to hide? What's your story?'*

Felicity noticed him waiting to be served, and he pointed to the coffee pot. She was purposefully dismissive, bantering with the locals behind him while she poured his coffee. He took it to a side table, took out his map and pen and started to ring timetables. She didn't notice him leave.

The following evening, Mabel, who was busy paying a tradesman, frowned at Felicity and nodded toward Bruno.

Reluctantly, Felicity walked over and asked him if he would like a drink.

He didn't look up. 'Coffee please, Ma-am.'

She glanced at him as he shuffled the brochures aimlessly. He looked lost and vulnerable. She felt ashamed; *'This is not how I should behave towards someone who has volunteered to leave his home to aid us with the war effort.'* She poured a cup for herself, took them over, and with a weak, forced smile, sat next to him.

He glanced into her eyes, *'Yes, they were grey.'* He saw her face flush and felt an urge to stroke it but held back. *'Why's she sending a "hands-off" signal?'*

64

Felicity coyly looked at him and felt uneasy, entirely exposed under his intense gaze. *'Who is this man?'* She drank her coffee with two hands to stop them from trembling.

While they studied the leaflets, each wanted to sketch their backgrounds. Bruno said, 'My group has just landed in Britain. I'm a chemist, dispensing medicines to the troops, which accounts for the difference in age from your usual clientele,' and pointed to the bar heaving with lively youngsters.

She said, 'My aunt and I have been running this for a few years now, helping the lads feel comfortable away from home. It's been a hectic time but a worthwhile cause.'

Bruno liked her soft voice, not weighted with the heavy accent he had heard in the city.

They joked together in a good pals' act, but the accidental touch of Bruno's hand was an electric shock that made her jump. She didn't trust herself to look into his eyes more than necessary.

'I'm ridiculous,' she thought. *'Have I joined the mindless little girls chasing the G.I.'s for nylons?'* It didn't stop her from imagining tracing his upper lip with her finger. Being close to him was thrilling, but also threatening in a way. She soon forgot the silliness and became engrossed in what he was saying.

Bruno passed a list to her. 'I'd like to visit these places and where my father lived before emigrating. He was born in Italy and came to England with his family during a slump. U.S. relatives then persuaded Pa to join them in the wine-making business.'

She studied the list, and he studied her, fascinated by her delicate unblemished, pale skin in contrast to the swarthiness of the Mediterranean women in his family. He quelled another urge to touch the opacity of her face. Despite his intense attraction, he would respect her unsaid wishes.

'My parents stayed here before they emigrated to the States. Their friends, the Cavallo's, didn't go. They joined family in running a restaurant here. I thought of locating them and giving them Pa's address. But now I'm here; it seems unrealistic with only their name as a clue to their whereabouts.'

Felicity tried to compose herself, but the club noise forced her to lean over and speak in his ear, 'I'll give it some thought.'

Bruno felt the warmth of her breath against his cheek, and it took all his self-control to remain impassive. He slowly handed her the scribbled note with the names of Lena and Ricardo Cavallo. As their hands touched, the heat from his skin sent shivers down her arm and down the back of her neck. He, too, experienced the electric charge between them.

She had to rise above these tantalising sensations, so she stood up and cheerily suggested, 'Come early tomorrow. Our plumber, Charlie, has always worked in the city. I'll ask Mabel, and we'll try to get hold of him.' She strolled towards the bar and dared not look back as she sensed he was a predator watching her.

He smiled to himself, he was suddenly very optimistic about being here. That touch of ours, *'Now that was something.'* He slipped out of the club into the darkness, leaving her to serve other customers. He was fascinated with her but wasn't quite sure why.

The following morning, Mabel rang Charlie and asked for help. He said, 'I know the cafe; it's now a specialist dry cleaner. They might know where the Italians went.' An hour later, he called back. 'The Cavallo's moved to Stockport; bought something in the High Street. Should be easy to track them down.'

Mabel said, 'That's a pint I owe you. I'll let you know if we find them.'

Bruno came into the club early, and Felicity was behind the bar. He pulled up a stool and ordered a beer to break the ice. He said, 'You were right. I had a great day out in Chester. So much to see. Those rows of black and white buildings wowed me; sure must be some age there.'

Felicity was upbeat, nervous to see him again. 'Yes, they're Tudor. I thought you'd like that enchanted place. I love the Victorian clock. Did you get to the cathedral? I must go back there now you've whetted my appetite.'

Pleased they were in tune with their banter; he said, 'As I walked around the walls, I could sense part of its Roman history.'

'It's like a magic spell.' They laughed together at these fanciful ideas.

He asked, 'Any news on the Cavallo's?'

'Yes, Mabel will fill you in.'

'You mean to say you found them? Boy, that was quick.'

Mabel came out of the office when she heard the accent. 'Hi Bruno. Charlie came up trumps and found the whereabouts of your friends. Stockport High Street. It's somewhere to try.'

'Where's Stockport?'

Mabel said, 'About half an hour on the bus.' She looked over at Felicity, struggling to serve as the bar filled up, so she waded in to help pull pints.

It was another busy night in the club, so Bruno left and told Mabel he would return to plan his next step; going to Stockport.

Bruno breezed in at seven the following evening.

'I've popped in before it gets busy.'

Mabel promptly placed two coffee mugs on the side table. Felicity saw him arrive but stopped herself from rushing over, feigned surprise, and then slowly went over to him with a welcoming smile.

He wanted to yell, *'Hey, Felicity! How can I get you out of here?'* He didn't because he might frighten her away. Instead he casually said, 'I'm going to Stockport tomorrow morning.' His approach to find out more about her was probably through Mabel. When Felicity went to serve customers, he took his chance, 'Does Felicity live with you?'

'Yes, she does. It is so convenient to have her and her two girls sharing the house.'

He smiled and digested, *'Two girls, but she's not mentioned a husband. He might be serving in the Forces.'*

The following morning, he turned up early at the club, determined not to pay special attention to Felicity.

She came bustling over, and he immediately noticed she had changed her look. Her blonde shoulder-length hair was loose, and there was a trace of red lipstick. Mesmerised, he sought the wedding ring on her finger. *'Why didn't I notice it before? Fancying married women is not my style. It is not fair to her; I must lay off.'*

He picked up the bus timetable and said, 'Half hourly services to Stockport. I've got something else to do today, I can go later in the week. Thanks for your help. I'll certainly let you know if I find them.' He left the club with a cheerful, 'So long, see you later.' It took all his willpower to stride away.

Felicity unhooked her overalls from behind the bar and dragged them on over her sapphire blue woollen dress. Mabel saw Felicity's disappointment at the rebuff, poured more coffee from the jug she had prepared for Bruno, and presented her niece with a sizeable mug.

She took it with a forced smile and thought, *'I shouldn't feel let down. He never even asked me to go. I was probably giving and receiving the wrong signals. The poor man was just being friendly; he'd said no words to suggest anything otherwise. It's my imagination that he fancies me.'*

She pretended not to see him when he arrived later than usual that evening. He requested, 'Small beer, please, Mabel.' He picked up the newspaper and located a quiet corner. With a forced blank expression, Felicity avoided direct eye contact but finally waved from afar as she collected glasses.

Bruno was relieved. *'Good. She's got the message,'* and stared at the newspaper without reading anything. He sat perplexed, *'Why did I get cold feet when I thought she was expecting me to ask her to help in my search? What's enticing me here night after night? Who's making me behave like a crazy hunter?'*

Felicity picked up her coat at ten o'clock. Demoralised, she needed to get out of the club. She said to Mabel, 'I'm tired, so I'll nip off home.'

Bruno approached the empty counter, 'Mabel, I saw Felicity leave. Is she dashing home to her husband?'

'Good heavens, No. She left him a few years ago and hasn't seen him since.'

Mabel was astonished that he turned abruptly and left without a word.

Chapter 16

Felicity trudged to the end of the street in time for an approaching tram. The driver waited long enough for her to sit in the entrance seat before he rang his loud bell to announce the departure.

Bruno sprinted the last few steps and leapt on. He overbalanced and sprawled into the space next to Felicity, landing with his face touching hers. A quick twist and his lips brushed hers for their first impromptu kiss. They sat in silence, both unsure whether or how to make conversation. They were thankful the driver interrupted the moment, 'Next stop Ardwick Green.'

'That's me,' she said. He took her hand and they jumped to the pavement. The bell sounded, and the tram rattled off like an old tin can being kicked down the road, taking its meagre light and clanking with it.

Felicity fumbled for the small torch in her pocket. In the gloom, she took his arm and pointed to their destination. He made out the vague outline of semi-detached houses on the other side of the green. The wide path cut through a canopy of trees that blocked out the residual light from the moon. The grass had been dead for years, but the evergreens thrived because copious rainfall washed the leaves, allowing them to breathe.

They followed the beam of light, which picked out old wooden seats and tree trunks, trip hazards in their progress to Mabel's house.

Unwilling to wait, they turned and clutched each other. Bruno's lips were soft as he searched for hers. They repeatedly kissed as they walked, stumbled up the steps, and entered the porch. He placed her against the side wall, slid off her cardigan, unzipped her dress at the side, and unhooked her bra, which caused her to shiver. He felt her breasts, and the dress crumpled around her feet.

She hurriedly slid her panties to her knees as he undid his flies, lifted her up and clumsily entered her. Waves of motion coursed down her thighs, and he held her tight against himself until this sensation repeated.

They gasped for breath, sweat trickling down their faces. This powerful surge had never happened to either of them, like tremors rocking the ground under their feet. Felicity savoured the overwhelming, all-consuming thrill.

Their bodies fused in the dark as they kissed and clung to each other. Eventually, Bruno stroked her face gently and eased himself away with a 'See you tomorrow, lovely Felicity. Sleep well,' and slipped her a folded handkerchief as he disappeared into the inky black of the overhanging branches.

It seemed sacrilege to use the torch, so she stepped out of her dress and located the keyhole with two hands. The key turned quickly, and she stumbled inside, closed the door, and rested her shaking body against it. She could hardly pull herself up the stairs. Her stomach churned as she washed away the residue of the stolen moment. She stored her clothes away neatly and looked at her comfortable winceyette nightie. She smiled at the following naughty thoughts. *'This is so unsexy. I'll have to get something more enticing.'*

As she lay in bed, she thought, *'What on earth have I done? I've just let a man I don't know take advantage of me. But I don't regret it. I'm just amazed that* at my age, *this gorgeous American makes me feel wanted and beautiful.'* She replayed the sensation of Bruno's strong arms lifting and supporting her. Engulfed in euphoria, she fell asleep.

The next day, Mabel was working at the club in their inner sanctum when she heard Bruno's voice. 'Good morning. Come on out. It's no use hiding.'

Mabel looked at her watch. *'It's only half past ten.'* She recognised who it was at once, 'Good morning Bruno. Papers are over there.'

'Thanks. Is Felicity coming in today?' he asked, trying to play it cool.

'Yes, any minute now.' She mused, *'Unusual early morning coffee time, asking for Felicity; he disappeared abruptly at the same time as her last night. Things are starting to add up.'*

Felicity swanned in, wearing a fitted emerald dress and navy cardigan and sauntered up to Bruno with a serene, enigmatic smile. She thought, *'How's he going to handle this?'*

Bruno, of course, had his opening gambit planned.

'Mabel, I fancied going out to the countryside for a breath of fresh air. Have you any ideas? I also wondered if you could spare Felicity for a few hours to show me around?'

'That's confirmed my suspicion.' Mabel thought.

Felicity said, 'Yes, Bruno. I'd love that. I miss the open landscape we had around Crewe,' and thought, *'Well done, mate. That was masterful, passing the buck to Mabel. Of course, knowing her, she's guessed by now.'*

Mabel said, No problem. Betsy loves to help out if I need her. Don't hurry back.' She intended no sarcasm, but she knew where this was leading. They didn't see her pursed lips and the shake of her head as they left.

Bruno tucked Felicity's arm over his when they were outside and said petulantly, 'Do we have to go to the countryside?'

'Yes. We'll catch the bus and find a country inn for lunch.' She winked at him conspiratorially.

He sighed with a false smile, 'Ma'am, that would be very nice.'

It took a change of buses to reach Wythenshawe Park. It covered many acres of well-kept gardens, a hall, buildings with attractions and a working farm. They methodically explored until they saw a pub tucked away in a secluded corner. They were grateful to rest their feet and eat the rationed salad, bread and cheese with a refreshing glass of cider.

On the threadbare window seat, they snuggled together, held hands and kissed, reminding them of last night's passion. They were silent on the bus on the return. Neither made a move until the terminus. He tried not to rush to the Regent, but his stride got faster and faster until she paused, breathless and laughing.

'I was never a good sprinter,' Felicity joked. 'Do you want to run on ahead?'

He locked the hotel bedroom door and stood with his back against it. The late afternoon sun filtered through the Victorian lace curtains as Felicity listened to the bustle of the market traders packing up. The couple edged slowly around the bed towards each other. He could see she was apprehensive, 'Alright?'

'I've never made love in the daylight before.'

'It's an acquired taste. You'll get used to it.' He made a playful grab for her, and they landed on the bouncy bed.

Kissing her lightly, he slowly undressed her. Then, with his mouth firmly on hers, he wriggled out of his clothes.

Shy at first, she kept her gaze fixed on his face until she had to close her eyes to eliminate any distraction that would interfere with the supreme tremors washing through her body.

He gasped as he collapsed on her, kissing her neck. With both of her legs clinging behind his back, she held onto him tightly, longing to stay locked to him forever.

They were awakened at seven in the evening by the lighting of street lamps. Felicity crept into the bathroom as he called out, 'There's no food rationing if you live next to a market. We usually get an excellent dinner here. Are you hungry?'

After a substantial pub meal, they chatted to the proprietor, making small talk until they both felt enough time had elapsed, and they couldn't resist the pressing urge anymore to resume their coupling.

In the bedroom, Bruno said, 'You look so sweet and vulnerable in that dress.' He unbuttoned it and led her to the bed. This time they were comfortable enough to explore more intimately, and after tender fondling and the natural rhythm of each other's bodies, they fell asleep.

The following morning, after breakfast, Bruno went to the club whilst Felicity returned home to change. Mabel was drinking tea in the kitchen. 'You didn't come back last night?'

Felicity blushed and raised her eyebrows, 'Bruno distracted me. Would it be alright if I took some time off? It's so quiet at the moment.'

Mabel ignored her better judgement, 'Yes, of course, why not take a week while you can?'

'Thanks. I've never met anyone like him.'

She watched Felicity float around doing the household chores and leave on cloud nine. She was pleased her niece was so distracted, dazed as though all reason had left her.

At the club, Mabel sat at the bar. She envied Felicity's newfound happiness and radiance, but as she stared wistfully into space, she thought, *'I have mixed feelings about this. The odds against it ending happily are sky-high. When the dream comes crashing down, at least she's had a whirlwind romance to tuck away in her box of memories.'*

Jenny bustled in with a bundle of letters and bills.

'Everything is unusually quiet again today. What's going on?' She grabbed a cup, emptied the coffeepot, and disappeared into the office.

Mabel said, 'I've given Felicity some time off.' She slid off the bar stool and picked up a duster.

Felicity met Bruno outside the club with a heartfelt hug and a wide smile. 'I've got a week's leave.' She felt wicked, like playing truant from school. An adventure into the unknown was happening. She felt safe and just wanted to be with him, always.

They waved at Mabel and, hand in hand walked to the tram. He said, 'Why don't we collect some of your clothes, take them to The Regent, and then I need to go shopping. If I'm hanging out with you all week, these are all I've got. My uniform's at the base.'

Swept up in the moment, Felicity said, 'A whole week to get to know each other.'

Bruno gave a sly smile, and she knew he was thinking precisely the same.

At home, Felicity invited Bruno in, 'Make a drink. You'll find everything in the kitchen, and I'll go pack.'

He noticed the stack of vouchers on the sideboard.

'What's all this about clothes coupons? I have a stash of them; a saleswoman rustled them up for me. I also have this wad of foreign pound notes to use up.'

'Oh, good idea.' She peeled some from the pile. 'Here, take mine. We've got loads; we're all machinists and make our clothes. It saves us a fortune.'

Within ten minutes she returned with a small, hard overnight case.

At The Regent, Bruno took up most of the bed in the compact double room and watched her unpack. She stowed dresses and shoes in the wardrobe, and underwear and stockings were neatly placed into a drawer. Toiletries were left in the bathroom and the plain cotton nightie came out last; she looked at it for a few seconds, whipped it up, folded and stowed it under the pillow.

He saw this action and thought, *'I agree, it is a bit homely but left to me, you won't be wearing it for any length of time.'* He smiled at his lascivious thoughts. Instead, he said, 'I hope this place is okay for you. I might have gone first class if I'd had warning I'd be entertaining.'

She curled up one side of her mouth in a lopsided grin and shrugged her shoulders. Bruno said, 'You really don't care, do you? I just want you to be happy.'

He leapt from the bed, and she dodged his outstretched hands and reached the door first. 'Some lunch, then shopping,' she said.

With his lustful thoughts dashed, he murmured, 'It was a good try, buster. You'll have to wait a little longer.'

They sat in the bar, ordered sandwiches and beer, and then strolled along the major shopping street. A stylish draper's shop tempted them in.

The elderly owner stood behind the counter where he'd started forty years ago. His assistants were away in the war, and he relished being useful again. *'Glad to be back. This retirement caper makes me feel old.'*

Bruno chose cotton underwear, a couple of striped traditional pyjama sets, trousers, shirts and a tie.

'Perhaps a couple of woollen sweaters, Sir? The North of England is probably not the climate you're used to.'

Felicity agreed and chose a crew neck and a V-neck to be added to the pile while Bruno counted out a few notes from his substantial wallet.

'Thank you, Sir. Here's your change. If you don't mind me reminding you, pickpockets are everywhere; perhaps your big notes should be in the hotel safe.'

'You're right. I've just started shopping. Thanks, I'll be careful.' He tried to signal and mime to Felicity, "How much should I tip?" She pulled out a couple of notes from his wallet and put them in Bruno's hand, ready for him to pass over.

'Thank you so much, Sir. I can deliver if you're staying locally.'

'That would be perfect. We're at The Regent.'

'Ah, just across the road. When these are packed, I'll drop the package over there, so you can carry on shopping unhindered. Is it Mr and Mrs?'

'Ponti. Thanks again, that will be great.' Bruno winked at Felicity.

He watched this fascinating couple walk away, holding hands. He prided himself on placing customers but was stumped with these. They were too old for first loves. *'I'll close for lunch and drop this package off.'*

His friend managed The Regent, and he took the receipt of the parcel, looked at the name, wrote the room number on it, and set it aside to be taken upstairs. 'I can offer you a pie and a cup of tea. There's also homemade cake.'

'That's just the ticket. I'll get us a table in the bar.'

Over lunch, his concierge friend said, 'You're dying to learn more about them, aren't you? I gather he's an American medic based in Warrington on leave for a few days. Probably here for the big push, which is the war secret everyone seems to know. As for her, she's Mabel's neice from Crewe. You remember Mabel who ran the Wellington Arms? She sent him round here. Nice chap! Life's got grim. I say let them have fun while they can.'

Satisfied with his friend's assessment, he returned to open the shop. *'I wonder who'll be my next intriguing customer?'*

Felicity gave Bruno a tour of the area until he said, 'I recognise where I am now. That's Exchange Station, where I get the train for Warrington.'

'Yes. This is one of the oldest sites in Manchester; shall we nip in for a drink.' The pub was cosy with its open fire; they settled down with a drink and a snack. They had forty years behind them in vastly different locations, and they would never run out of topics to compare and discuss. On their stroll back to the hotel, Bruno suddenly stopped and pulled her inside a department store. 'I refuse to wear my new clothes until you've got something.'

He called the lift and pressed the Ladies' Clothes Department button. As they got out, a young assistant sprang forward and ushered them to her counter.

'Yes, sir? How can I assist you?'

He was apprehensive. *'Gosh, this could be tricky. I've no idea how to go about buying a negligee. Felicity seems proud and sensitive. I just want to spoil her, not make her feel cheap, but I've lost her if this goes wrong. Here's a confident-looking assistant. I'll follow her lead.'*

Bruno winked at Felicity and asked the saleslady. 'Can you show us some negligees, please? Glamorous ones.'

The girl didn't betray her surprise. She glanced at Felicity to gauge her size, took two boxes down from behind her, unwrapped them from their tissue papers, and draped them reverently over the counter.

Felicity gasped at their breath-taking beauty. One was pink lace and silk, not sluttish, just a classic. The other was delicate blue satin, plain but with a superb bias cut to skim fluidly down the body to the fluted hem. She marvelled at the material and the artistry as the girl discreetly showed her the size. Felicity nodded quickly with embarrassment.

Bruno stepped forward. 'Very nice. We'll have both. OK, Honey?'

Felicity stuttered, 'They're beautiful.' At no point was a price mentioned, although he waved the ticket away with no consequence when the sales assistant showed him. She thought, 'This is right out of my league. I don't know how to behave. I feel gauche and cheap.' She kept quiet until she realised it was solely a transaction between Bruno and the assistant.

After years of penny-pinching, buying something without caring about the price was shocking. The beautiful garments which were now hers to wear had an effect. She felt special, ready to ignore connotations of a kept woman or floozy. Like play-acting, she behaved as though this luxury shopping was the norm and, for five minutes, stepped into a new world.

He was enjoying the fun and gazed at her adoringly, so she stood tall, acted glamorous and was loved.

He pointed, 'Hey! Look at those pink fluffy slippers.'

The girl brought them over and asked Felicity, 'Size six?'

'Yes, thank you.' She slipped them on and gave a twirl. 'They fit perfectly. More Hollywood than Manchester, but I love them.'

The sales assistant set to work, wrapping with the massive amounts of tissue paper and ribbons the items deserved. She ensured her clients enjoyed the professional performance, knowing the floor manager was watching in the background. She handed over their parcels, led them to the lift, pressed the down button and backed away as if they were royalty.

Minutes later, the floor manager passed her counter, smiled and nodded, a rare occurrence on his floor. He noted, *'This one has style and can be trusted with future special customers.'*

The assistant waited until the coast was clear and pulled out the brand-new crisp banknote Bruno had slipped into her top pocket. She popped it into her purse, thankful it doubled her weekly wages. She smiled, *'Goodness. I never dreamed I would get rid of those nighties until the war was over.'*

At The Regent, they unpacked their boxes, and Bruno found the drapers' complimentary card with a small presentation case. It contained enamel cufflinks, an inexpensive but elegant touch.

He said, 'Everybody gained today.' She smiled at him in the mirror as he looked over at a grey-lace vision brushing her blonde hair. 'Especially me.'

Later in their hotel room, Bruno and Felicity, compelled to touch each other, assured themselves that this relationship was genuine. There was an unspoken urgency to savour every moment together, suppressing the reality that he would leave the following week. The intensity of their passion was overwhelming.

Over the following days, they dared to dream and plan a future together in America. They yearned for this closeness to remain, and both inwardly believed their relationship would last.

Bruno said, 'We're together now; found each other at last. Every minute must count.'

In a moment of sanity, Felicity said, 'What about the girls?'

'What about the girls?' he asked.

'I don't want to leave them behind. When I left Crewe, I hadn't expected to bring them into a war zone, but they do seem happier here.'

Felicity didn't worry too much about their long-term futures. They were content with their jobs and found half-decent boyfriends and a social life. Betsy now worked in a factory, specialising in sewing men's evening-dress trousers. It was a wise choice; they would always be in demand.

Bruno seemed to have a tacit understanding with Mabel. From her directness, she implied, 'Be kind to my niece, or I will kill you.'

They spent the first day at a vast amusement park, Belle Vue, where the zoo housed and cared for endangered tropical animals and exotic species; lions, tigers and even monkeys.

The elephant ride caused hysterical laughter as the keeper strapped them to a wooden contraption like a park bench on its back. The elephant lumbered away with the movement throwing them from side to side. When they dismounted from their tour, Bruno stood eye to eye with the giant and couln't help but stroke its trunk, running his fingers over the crevices of the grey crepey skin.

As a tip, he handed a pound note to the keeper, 'Can we feed it?'

The keeper gave him an unpeeled banana. Bruno held one out. 'Here you go. Thanks for the ride.' The elephant gratefully wrapped its swinging trunk around the afternoon treat and pushed it into its mouth.

Felicity moved at Bruno's caring touch, kissed his cheek, and squeezed his arm. They continued their walk. The refreshment area led to the entertainment park, dominated by slides and roundabouts. They held hands as they whizzed around in a carriage on the big dipper that towered above the region, perched high on rails that pelted around at speed, full of screaming, terrified families. They came off this ride, laughing so much that their jelly legs hardly supported them.

A small, quiet restaurant gave them respite from the hubbub of excited people. Over dinner, he filled in more about his background. 'I had a promising career in research in New York but was tired of the bustling East Coast life by the time I qualified as an analytical chemist. Pa annexed part of the main building for a laboratory at home because I wanted to study grape types and blends for the business side. I'm an Italian country boy at heart. I felt lucky to be working at home.'

Felicity loved hearing about his life and urged him to continue.

'I'm the unmarried one of three brothers, and we thought one of us should support the war effort, so here I am.'

'That's an enormous commitment. Just because you're not married.'

'Yes, but it led me to you.' he said, reaching over the table and clasping her hands in his. 'Before settling down together, I would love to show you the Veneto in Northern Italy, where my family originated. It is beautiful; you will love it.'

'That would be incredible. My own Italian tour guide.'

'To prepare for our life together, why don't you learn a bit of the language?'

'Si.' she said.

After dinner, the sound of up-tempo music tempted them into the lovely dance hall. The gallery, lined with exterior walkways and balustrades, had a few steps that invited you down to the sunken floor. Discreet lighting and plush carpets added to the air of luxury. The professional five-piece band with a resident singer had a broad repertoire to ensure an enjoyable evening for countrywide visitors.

Bruno was so impressed to find such old-fashioned charm amid a noisy amusement park and zoo. They watched the male dancer leap ahead onto the dance floor and help down his partner, who responded by lightly skipping down the steps, one hand firmly in his, the other holding out her full skirt at the side. As the music started, they twirled across the sprung dance floor with its glacial wooden surface, a real privilege for the serious dancers.

The couple found enough energy and steps in common to dance to a few well-known tunes. They found a dark corner, grabbed each other, smooched, and welded together until they decided they needed to continue their fondling back in the privacy of their hotel room.

On the bus returning to their hotel, they propped up against each other, tired and happy, anticipating a continuation of their love affair behind closed doors.

They were asleep when the warning siren wailed eerily. Automatically, Bruno propped himself up on one elbow, then disentangled himself from her clutches and whispered the current catchphrase, 'Don't you know there's a war on?'

She gave a wry smile, but her daughters and Mabel were only half a mile away, and worried thoughts engulfed her as she slipped her nightie on and covered it with her overcoat. Half-dressed, bleary-eyed guests and workers trooped downstairs to the shared reinforced basements, where makeshift beds and blankets were ready. War can be a great leveller; mink coats snuggled down amongst the hotel staff's uniforms.

With a steady, triumphant tone, the all-clear tore through the night. This signal was sometimes just a suggestion because as stray bombers limped away from the armada in the sky, they jettisoned their unused bombs to lighten their load. Sadly, it was Russian roulette where they landed. Some only damaged vegetables in the open fields, while others destroyed town buildings.

Felicity sat on the edge of the bed, stretching and yawning, recovering from the brief night break. Market trading started at dawn, but only a slight noise of the bustle and activity from the market stalls below reached their cosy room. She leaned over to pick up her earrings from the bedside table and picked up Bruno's dog tags.

'Why have they got notches top and bottom?'

'Too gruesome to tell you.' he said.

'Now you've raised my curiosity. You've really got to tell me.'

'OK, but only if you come back to bed.' With Bruno's serious face close to hers, he began, 'When a soldier dies in battle, before his body is collected, they use the notch in the dog tag to hold his jaw open over his teeth, top and bottom. Another soldier would kick his jaw shut, embedding it in place, ensuring identification when the body returned home.'

Felicity's face filled with horror; she wrinkled her nose with disgust and scrambled out of bed towards the shower, hoping the hot running water might erase the bleak scene in her mind.

After dressing, Bruno was more aware of the pinch of the chain around his neck and the cold metal against his chest. He took her arm and hurried her to the small dining room, knowing that a bright atmosphere at breakfast would lift their moods. He hoped that if he enthused over the day's plans, he would distract her from the horrific images of battlefield carnage.

During the week, Bruno and Felicity met up with Anna, Betsy and Mabel at the Club. The effect this man had on their mother astounded them. Like a flower, she had opened and revealed her delicate beauty. They had never seen her smile so much.

Felicity's worries about Bruno being accepted were unfounded. He bowled them over and charmed them with his calm manner and good looks. It also helped that bribes from Warrington were available to him. 'Some little gifts from the canteen,' he drawled, casually handing over coffee, lipsticks and perfume.

A few days ago, she had impressed him with Belle Vue. Today, she would surprise him with a visit to Blackpool, the largest Lancashire resort, perched on a long sandy beach. The tide retreated a long way and took hours to return.

They alighted the train before the city centre to get the full impact of the tower viewed from the beach. It resembled a giant lighthouse; steel ladders formed the sides, reaching a lookout area. Everyone who visited Blackpool could view the structure from miles away because of the surrounding flat countryside. Its base housed a vast dance floor with a remarkable organ that dominated the entertainment centre. It was an exciting introduction to an evening of dancing and frivolity when the organ rose from the floor and played lively tunes to lure the waiting pairs to dance.

Like other visitors paddling in the sea, he rolled up his trousers to his knees, carried his shoes, and strolled along the shoreline, holding her free hand.

They ate a sandwich lunch on the promenade enjoying the beach scene below, the flat miles of clean sand with families grouped around their canvas deckchairs. Day-trippers relished the clean air and smell of the sea as they splashed far from the city grime.

Out of the blue, he suggested, 'I've never seen such an original and unique place. Wouldn't it be fun to come back for a couple of days on our honeymoon?'

'Oh, Yes!' she squealed, accepting his early proposal. All the surrounding sounds faded for a second, and they smiled at each other, their future assured. 'We have time to take in the Tower Ballroom.'

Bruno got the flavour of the atmosphere. He said, 'You people are serious dancers.'

She skipped, 'Like singing. It's free for everyone.'

Most shops closed in Manchester for Wakes Week, a holiday period, originally a religious celebration or feast, particularly in North-West England during the Industrial Revolution. Visitors from the working centres invaded the resort en masse and stayed in the stark terraces of three-storied identical grand-fronted buildings. The only difference was the sizeable ornamental name board outside each one. If you forgot the name of your boarding house, it was a seaside jungle that you had to negotiate. The budget boarding houses were called fanciful and amusing names, such as Beau Sejour, Tropicana and Villa Mirage, which were not truthful descriptions by anyone's stretch of the imagination.

She told him legendary stories about the dragon landladies. 'All lights switched off at ten. Queues formed at the only bathroom on each floor, but lines moved quickly if families went in together. Breakfast must be over by 9.45 am, and the doors locked until 5.00 pm when it opened for evening meals.'

These boarding houses were ultra-clean and respectable, with ample, wholesome food ready to be devoured after unaccustomed fresh sea air for the whole day.

They had built huge shelters on the roadside on the slope to the beach, a Godsend on rainy days. Wartime had sadly altered the look, fun, and vibrancy. Felicity expected to see more of the bucket and spade contingent, but it was autumn, and the crowds of noisy, vibrant children were missing.

A brass band startled Felicity and Bruno. They played booming military marching music and hurried to the roadside to watch them. To their astonishment, they saw a small troupe of soldiers. Dressed in mismatched sizes of brand-new air force blue uniforms, they played various brass instruments, banged drums and tried hard to march in time along the road. A few local children mimicked them, dancing along the pavement. The music faded away as the band turned onto a side road.

They strolled back to the beach and stopped outside a bus shelter. An elderly couple shifted along the wooden seat, making space.

'Thanks, but we're not catching a bus; we're getting the train', Felicity said.

The wizened man pulled off his flat cap and pointed behind the hotels. 'Did you like the marching band? The RAF training ground and airstrip are over there, behind the town. We spoke to a young recruit who had volunteered. He usually played weekends in a beat group and told us his mum and dad would have died laughing to see him, a fully-fledged guitarist, all dressed up, just tinkling on a triangle.'

His nosy wife tightened her headscarf. 'Are you here on holiday?'

Felicity smiled politely. 'Only on a day trip. I live in Manchester and always find it worth coming to the seaside to have the city cobwebs blown away.' She lightly squeezed Bruno's hand, signalling the time to leave.

'Been nice to meet y'all,' Bruno said.

The old lady's mouth dropped open at the American accent, and she watched the couple as they strolled off hand in hand. 'Ooh, what a lovely-looking couple,' she sighed. 'You can tell they're in new love.'

'Stop being so mushy, you old romantic,' the gent said, then picked up his wife's veined and wrinkly hand and kissed it hard.

The empty train to Manchester chugged along. Bruno slipped off his shoes and propped his feet on the seat opposite. He said, 'I feel a wreck, and my face is plastered in salt and sand. I can taste it.'

Felicity said, 'That's exactly how you should feel after a day in Blackpool.' She examined his right hand and traced lines across it. 'Hey, this is interesting. You have a long lifeline. Look how it curves around your thumb. Your head line is simple, but it has a break.'

'Will I meet a tall, dark stranger?' he joked.

'Silly, you are the tall, dark stranger.' She kissed his sand-ridden forehead and continued to study his hand. 'Slim, straight fingers show that you are an idealist and a planner. The love line swoops under the index finger. You will follow your heart and always marry for love. Ooh, you are very sensual.'

He said, 'Where did you find that?' She looked to the sky, and he realised he was being teased. She kissed his palm and waited for the expected return kiss. With her feet tucked up sideways, she leaned against his shoulder.

'Ain't this something,' Bruno said and pointed to the Victorian architecture as the train approached Manchester's London Road Station. Sadly, minor bomb damage had occurred, mainly from strays. The enemy targeted strategic areas outside the centre, like armament factories, docks, and railways.

Felicity nodded and looked at the buildings, aware they hid their genuine magnificence under layers of soot built up over decades. She wondered what fate had in store for her and clasped Bruno's firm hand for reassurance.

She broke the melancholy by suggesting, 'Let's see if we can locate the Cavallo's tomorrow.'

The following day, after a short bus ride, they quickly found his father's friends, Lena and Ricardo, in Stockport, who greeted them with hugs and back-slapping as if they were meeting up with close family. They were not expecting a visit from a G.I., especially the son of their long-standing friends, Eva and Carlo.

Bruno asked Ricardo, 'Why did you leave Manchester?'

'After our two boys were born, city life became inconvenient, and this cafe was on the market. We could afford to buy this plus a cottage. Today's Sunday, so we'll close early and take you for a drive into the country towards Macclesfield. We'll go back to our house for tea.'

Bruno updated them on his parent's successful emigration and integration into winemaking.

Lena said to Felicity, 'What a lovely surprise to hear about Carlo and Eva. After all these years, we often wondered what happened to them.'

At the Cavallo's house, Ricardo showed Felicity his sizeable vegetable patch when she showed an interest in gardening. It gave Lena a chance to ask Bruno a few questions.

'How did you meet Felicity, and have you known her long?'

'I met her at a serviceman's club in the city. She's separated from her husband and has two teenage daughters. She's adorable. I haven't known her long, but I'll buy an engagement ring to show I'm serious next time I come on leave. Do you think a single diamond would be suitable for her?'

Lena looked at his earnest face, 'A solitaire is always acceptable, but with quality diamonds, the size matters too.' They laughed together like conspirators as the others joined them from the garden.

After exchanging addresses and promises to keep in contact, they dropped Bruno and Felicity back into the town.

On their last evening in the hotel room, the couple undressed hurriedly, eager to continue their enjoyment of each other's bodies. Their lovemaking had an underlying tinge of sadness, as they were both aware of the limited time before Bruno joined his company in Warrington. Seven days had slipped by too soon. Tomorrow they had to tear themselves away from each other. She took in his reflected chiselled features as he stared out the window. They both knew every moment of this week was precious, to be stored in their memories.

Chapter 17

It was a mild Sunday morning, and Mabel and the girls greeted Bruno and Felicity. He pointed to his case, 'My uniform is at the base. Is it alright if I leave this full of civvies for my next leave?' With affirmation from Felicity, he bounded upstairs and stored the holdall at the bottom of her wardrobe.

Mabel unpacked the paper shopping bag, delighted to see Bruno had bribed a butcher and bought fillet steak, salad and a bottle of wine. It was a treat to have steak; she'd not seen it in a long time.

She hunted around for wine glasses and found five mismatched ones. *'Better than tumblers. I wonder if there are any spare glasses at the club? I'll get some good ones for the next time he eats here.'* She then realised what she'd thought, *'The next time. I truly hope there will be one.'*

She made a concerted effort to push the sad thoughts away as she prepared the sizeable green salad. Bruno opened the wine and wafted the cork under his nose.

The girls extended the large wooden table in the living room to seat six and laid it with Mabel's special handmade lace tablecloth.

The ladies raved over the wine as he poured it with a flourish, even though it had a bitter taste after drinking their usual port and lemonade on high days and holidays.

Bruno said, 'My family in California is in the wine business.' and loosely translated the label. They followed his lead and lifted their glasses to see the deep burgundy colour and feigned enthusiasm.

Betsy asked, 'Is it a big vineyard? Do the grapes hang down from wires?' trying to sound knowledgeable.

He laughed. 'You'd be very disappointed. We have several enormous fields with rows of small bushes. We plant a white or red rose at the end of each row of vines to show whether we make red or white wine from those grapes.'

She looked at Bruno, enthralled with the prospect of visiting such a sight. 'It must look beautiful.'

'Well, that's the tourist version. They're actually planted as a clever early warning system. Roses attract aphids, black rot or mildew before they reach the vines. This early detection stops them from spreading to the grapes. The rose thorns at the end of each row ensured the working animals, oxen or draft horses, turned correctly and weren't tempted to cut corners and damage the vines.'

Betsy said, 'This is fascinating. I don't know any of this stuff. I would love to hear more.'

He continued to enthral his audience, 'If they keep the bushes low, they make beautiful snaking patterns as they follow the contours of the hills. Even the little stone buildings peering from the hillside are well disguised. He looked over at Felicity and winked. You must come over and see it all for yourselves.'

They sat mesmerised by Bruno's evocative description of his home. No one wanted him to stop, so he didn't.

'When Pa inherited the property from his family, he built three houses on one side, next to a building for offices and a showroom. Pa, Ma and we three boys lived in one until we moved out to get married. But I was still at University, going backwards and forwards to New York. It made sense to let Steve, the Manager, rent mine. He's ready to retire soon.'

Mabel had misgivings. *'It's a little too soon to invite us all to California. He must be serious about Felicity.'*

As they went through the motions of savouring their wine, Mabel leaned toward Bruno. 'Will it be difficult if you get drafted to fight in Italy?'

Felicity turned to Mabel and frowned at her, shaking her head, not wishing to introduce a heavy or controversial topic during their last meal.

Bruno said, 'No, it's a valid and interesting question.' He turned to Mabel and gave her his full attention. He said, 'The recruitment staff covered it when I enlisted. They said, as a non-combatant medic, it would not arise. They asked if I would help as an interpreter with any injured or captured Italians. I assured them I'd be delighted to help with language or other difficulties.'

There was a momentary silence; they all realised the gravity of the actions which might lie ahead. The wall clock showed four, and Bruno stood up slowly and solemnly and looked at Felicity.

Their hearts sank as Betsy and Anna sensed the significance of this occasion for their mother. They had accepted this handsome, wonderful man into their lives without reservation. Unable to speak, they both hugged him and hurried away. Wartime parting had to be borne bravely to lessen the heartache for everyone.

Bruno had said that train-side farewells were harrowing and suggested that Felicity remain at home to weep privately. As they clung to each other in the hallway, he assured her, 'I will write often. I've treasured this time with you, my darling Felicity, and will return as soon as possible.'

Felicity held his face and gazed into his dark eyes that became blurred, 'Please stay safe and always remember that I love you.' She kissed him fervently and turned away. A faint, 'I love you too.' were his last words she heard as she stumbled towards her bedroom.

Her heart pounded as she closed the door, and she could only catch every other breath. To calm herself, she lay face down on the bed. A soft whimpering into the pillows turned into a full howl, deep and hurting like a wounded wolf.

At the front door, Mabel looked at Bruno, who clenched his lips together in a valiant effort to stay composed. *'These are unusual times,'* she thought, *'Everything magnified and poignant; better let them suffer the sad parting. They've been sheltered in a bubble of love and excitement, which has just burst.'*

He hesitated, turned on the top step, and clasped her hands in his. 'Mabel, please treasure Felicity for me until I come back. Thank you so much for your friendship.'

The only response she could muster was a firm nod as the tears silently rolled down her face as she watched him stride head high across Ardwick Green towards the bus stop.

Mabel slowly shut the front door and leaned against the cold hall wall. Seeing an anguished white face reflected in the hall mirror shocked her. *'I must be strong for her; Felicity mustn't see me like this.'*

Chapter 18

Day after day, week after week, Felicity watched for the postman for any news from Bruno. No letter came, nothing! Disillusioned, she finally stopped looking; it was too punishing.

She thought, *'I've fooled myself. I'm far too old to join the G.I. brides on their way to an idyll in the States. I must have been out of my mind.'*

It had just been a week of wonderful madness, which brought her alive and promised so much, only to dash her down. Felicity felt drained of life. How had she been so easily turned? Hope vanished.

Seeing Felicity so forlorn, Mabel said to the girls, 'I feel guilty for encouraging Bruno. We were all hoodwinked.'

Betsy said, 'We wanted this dream for her so much that we became emotionally invested, too. Let's face it; he was handsome and charming.'

Mabel was approaching sixty, the clientele was lessening, and she urgently needed to prepare for her old age. She dreamt of the cliché, a cottage in the country. To her, this meant a house with a large garden in a leafy suburb.

It wasn't long before an advertisement in the newspaper caught her attention. She wasted no time arranging a viewing of the four-bedroom house in Marple, a few miles from the city.

She booked taxis both ways and met the owners one afternoon. They had moved out before the war and wanted a quick sale. For years, the house lay empty. It was formerly a smallholding surrounded by a large garden. The peeling paintwork, ramshackle outbuildings and overgrown weeds had put prospective buyers off. But Mabel was intrepid, had the foresight of what it could become, and had tackled far worse. She also had a willing team of reliable workmen who would relish working in the clean air and countryside.

She gingerly stepped amongst the brambles and purple thistles, trying to reach the outhouses. On her return to the vendors sitting on a rickety bench near the front door, she glanced at her sleeves; white fluff balls clung all over them. She roared with laughter. 'Now I know why you named it Thistledown Farm.'

The vendors had taken to Mabel and her enthusiasm for traipsing around their property. He said, 'It looks like you love this place as much as we did.'

As she stood and picked off the thistles and flicked them away, she said, 'Yes, it's in a wonderful location, but it needs so much love and care to return it to a family home. Is it possible to rent out the pigsties and let sheep graze?' Mabel's aspiration, first envisaged with her fiancé, was uppermost in her thoughts.

'Oh, I'm sure the farmers will soon be knocking on your door to rent some land.'

'It's exactly what I'm looking for, but I'm not sure I can afford the house plus what it needs to bring it back to life. Thank you so much for seeing me this afternoon.' She turned to walk down the path to the waiting taxi.

The elderly gentleman took his wife's hand, looked at her and winked. She nodded, smiled back, and he called out, 'Miss Evans, please wait a minute.'

Mabel stopped and turned, ready to offer a hand if they needed help getting off the seat.

'My wife and I wonder what can you offer us that leaves you enough to do it up?'

She was put on the spot but sensed that the couple might accept a low offer. She quickly calculated a ballpark figure for renovations and added half the property's price. With the profit made from the club, she could just about buy it outright. Her hands sweated in her pockets. Her pipe dream was within reach, and her heart fluttered as she submitted a verbal proposal and waited.

'May I talk to my wife alone for a minute?' he asked.

'Of course.' Mabel stepped away and walked to the garden gate. A robin swooped down and trilled at her as she admired the view. She gasped, 'Oh my! You're the symbol of new beginnings.'

The couple had tottered within earshot, and the wife said, 'Yes, indeed it is; a promising start to your new life here.'

The gentleman said, 'We want you to have it and are delighted to accept your offer.'

Mabel didn't know what to do, whether to hug the frail couple, shake their hands or kiss them. She needn't have worried; the gentleman clasped her hands in his, then slowly pointed to the battered double-door shed. 'All the tools you'll ever need are in there. Please take it all with our blessings. We know everything's in your safe hands.'

He opened the gate, led his wife to their car and left Mabel, dabbing her eyes with a handkerchief, standing on the path.

Chapter 19

Felicity and the girls were all agog, listening to Mabel's exploits. They made plans to visit at the weekend. The sale was completed without a hitch, and Mabel revelled in starting another renovation project.

Anna and Betsy visited as often as possible, bringing boyfriends and other willing muscle power for carting or painting. Friends who had previously benefitted from Mabel's kindness found a perfect chance to repay her and spent a healthy few hours out of doors tackling the garden wasteland. It was always a relaxed day out and delivered a great sense of achievement.

Felicity found herself as the official gardener; experience with her small garden in Crewe gave her an excellent background to start on this one. To her delight, they unearthed established paths and concrete bases under the weeds and debris, suitable to site further sheds or create seating areas. Gifts of apple trees and surplus vegetables were welcome additions and started the kitchen garden.

The vendor was right; as soon as work began on the outhouses, the neighbouring farmers introduced themselves, nosy about what was happening. She agreed on rental terms and soon walked amongst a few grazing sheep, cows and pigs.

On completion of the renovation, Mabel's retirement plans returned to centre stage. The club was coming to the end of its usefulness and had served its purpose. It had been a success; countless young men away from home had found warmth and a welcome.

Mabel said to Felicity, 'We should be proud of our achievements. Fewer customers are coming, and I want to retire now the house in Marple is ready. As you'll be taking it over, any thoughts about what kind of club you want to run? Perhaps we can discuss possibilities or sell it to a developer?'

'It lends itself to be used for musical entertainment, possibly a nightclub. That's what today's clientele are asking for.'

'That sounds really good. I'll keep my stake in it then.'

They were clearing up behind the bar when two officious-looking, burly men dressed in heavy dark coats came up to the counter and displayed their identity cards.

'Home Office; may we have a moment? I'm Detective Watts, and this is Detective Jenkins.'

'Can I get you some tea?' Mabel asked.

They looked at each other and nodded. 'That would be really nice. Thank you.'

Felicity and Mabel sat opposite them. Felicity noticed that Mabel seemed anxious. *This looks more serious than a law infringement or outstanding debt.'*

Detective Jenkins started, 'An American officer has gone AWOL, absent without leave. It's a serious offence. Their military police were assigned but had no success tracing him, so they passed it over to us.'

Felicity glanced at Mabel; they instinctively knew what this was about.

From his notebook, Detective Watts read, 'His fellow officers said he frequented this club when on leave in Manchester. His name is Lieutenant Bruno Ponti.'

Felicity let out a little exclamation at his name.

Mabel's mouth opened wide, 'Oh my God, we know Bruno!'

'We're treating his disappearance as suspicious as he has not accessed his bank account, and his passport and official papers are still in Warrington. His company left for Europe without him.'

Felicity sat still, pale and expressionless, unable to process this unsettling information.

'Apparently, this is completely out of character. We're stumped too.'

Tears filled Felicity's eyes, but she turned away so they couldn't see. She was not expecting this sort of news, not today, never!

Mabel said, 'So he's disappeared without a trace?'

'Yes, Madam. Any ideas where he might have gone?'

Felicity couldn't speak, so Mabel said, 'No. We all thought he had gone to Europe with his troop.'

She touched Felicity to stay in her seat and escorted the two men out. 'We had become friends with him. He told us he was coming here on his next leave and left some clothes with us. We thought it strange that we'd heard nothing from him yet. Please let us know if you find him or anything else?' She nodded decisively towards Felicity and raised her eyebrows, and the two men immediately understood why.

After they left, Felicity, ashen-faced, looked at Mabel. 'I need a stiff drink.'

'Me too.' Mabel replied and busied herself behind the counter.

Anna and Betsy had seen the two uniformed men leave. Betsy said, 'What was that all about? What are you doing, drinking so early?'

'Sit down, girls.' Mabel said in a solemn voice. 'Bruno's gone missing; they were the police investigating the case.'

They hurried over and cuddled their mother. Every kind of scenario played out in their minds. They fervently wanted to believe Mabel, who said, 'He didn't write because he couldn't.'

The girls wanted to live with that idea rather than think he had dumped their mother. They exchanged puzzled glances for a few days, shaken at this development, but found nothing to discuss. It was a complete mystery. He'd vanished.

Felicity was heartbroken. She carried on working, but with no joy in her steps. His disappearance had taken the wind out of her sails, and she felt rudderless and completely adrift.

Time passed slowly; every day, she waited, still hoping for a letter or any sign from Bruno. She gradually moved on from sorrow and now scolded herself for being so gullible, so naïve. Like a star-struck schoolgirl, he had dazzled her. She didn't know what to think anymore, alternating from desolation to fervent hopefulness. Until they heard with certainty, there was a chance he would turn up, but would he be dead or alive?

Chapter 20

After the Home Office visit, Felicity looked through Bruno's belongings in the large holdall. A few small photos fell out. Most of them were his close family she had already seen. Then she came across one picture she hadn't noticed; a snap of a dark-haired boy. She looked fondly at the child, who resembled Bruno. Neatly written in Italian on the reverse was "Al Caro Papa. Con affetto da Edoardo." She roughly interpreted it as, "To darling Papa. With love from Edoardo." Judging by the boy's age in the picture, an adult had written it. She slumped onto the bed; the shock of this discovery brought on nausea she'd been suffering all week.

She replayed the scene when she asked him if he was married. He replied, 'No. I had two long-term relationships, which fizzled out. One was when I was in college, training to be a chemist. She had someone else by the time I came back home. The second was almost the same scenario. Being interested in viniculture, my parents paid for my course at university. I wanted to take a science degree and apply the knowledge to their winery business. I became more excited by higher education than by her.'

She remembered he'd shrugged and said, "It's a close community where I live, and I'm still friends with them and their husbands. I have no entanglements." Followed by, "I know about your husband's betrayal; Betsy told me."' Felicity replaced the photographs, zipped up the bag and slammed it into the corner, ready to be stowed in the loft. She was livid; *'No entanglements indeed. Who's this in the photo, then? He's probably another liar, but I'll keep this to myself. I won't see him again, anyway.'*

Anger replaced her foolish thoughts; not only had she lost the man, but he'd shattered the entire dream scenario he'd painted - a picture of living a lush life in the sunshine and world travel. It sounded like a fairy-tale, which is precisely what it turned out to be.

Felicity felt upset and sickly for the following few days and attributed it to emotional disruption. After she threw up one morning, she knew the sign; it confirmed she was pregnant. Her first reaction was disbelief. She was thirty-nine and would be an older mother, but she knew she was keeping it. The next hurdle would be conveying this astonishing news to the family.

Chapter 21

Felicity chose a Saturday breakfast time when everyone was sitting at the table, planning their day. She thought she might lose her news in their enthusiasm, but who was she kidding?

She walked in, unusually late for her breakfast. Betsy looked up, 'Mum, are you alright? You look very pale.'

'Thank you, I'm fine. Just pregnant,' and sighed in resignation and joined them.

Anna threw down her magazine. 'What! You must be joking?'

Felicity looked down, embarrassed under the scrutiny of her daughters' gazes.

With a raised, belligerent voice, Anna said, 'Bruno's missing, and you're having a baby? Am I dreaming - has the world gone mad?' She stood up, red-faced and angry, 'Mum, after all you've said to us about being careful, taking precautions. I can't believe you'd be so stupid.'

Betsy looked on, frozen-faced, too shocked to comment.

Felicity stood up to them. 'I know, I know. He just swept me off my feet; I'd dismissed the possibility of pregnancy at my age. How wrong I was.'

Mabel, of course, had guessed. She'd seen the pasty-faced, off-her-food Felicity before and had already mulled over several scenarios. She was initially worried that her niece might be ill until she accidentally saw her counting the days on the kitchen calendar.

She visualised an angry scene brewing and interrupted. 'Think about the difference this makes to our plans.' She had their full attention. 'I'm retiring anyway, but we can sell the club instead of Felicity running it as an entertainment centre. Who wants this baby growing up in the centre of a busy city? Thistledown is ready and waiting, and I've never had a baby to look after, so I'd love it if Felicity moved in with me.'

The girls were shame-faced, and Anna stuttered, 'It was just such a shock. Of course, you're right. You must go to the countryside, mum.'

Now in full flow, Mabel carried on with another suggestion. 'Marple is too far out to commute, so you girls will have to rent a flat in the city. On the other hand, there's plenty of space at the cottage. You'd be very welcome, have your own rooms, and there's plenty of work in Stockport.'

Anna and Betsy looked favourably on this bright side, and their thunderous faces softened.

Felicity smiled gratefully at her aunt for not criticizing her, summing it up and clarifying the situation. Two young heads were now close in consultation. Judging by the brief time it took and the broad smiles on their faces, it was good news.

Mabel said, 'Whatever you decide will be alright with me. There's no hurry.' She smiled. 'After all, you've months to decide!' The atmosphere lightened when the humour started.

Anna said, 'Of course, we're coming with you. It'll be lovely for all of us. If you're going to live it up in the country, so are we! You can't have all the fun.'

Betsy chimed in, 'Can we get a dog now, Auntie?'

'Of course!' said Mabel. 'What kind do you want?'

Anna and Betsy had definite ideas. 'Spaniels are not too big,' said Anna, already savouring thoughts of grooming the silky fur. Betsy agreed with her usual foresight, 'If we get a puppy now, I'll ensure it is fully trained for when the baby arrives.'

Mabel felt the calm in the room and enjoyed listening to her three beloved girls chatting and making plans. *'Everything's going to be okay,'* and put the kettle on for the comforting ritual of four cups of tea.

There was a striking contrast between Manchester city centre and Marple, a small village on the outskirts. Felicity initially envisaged the city to have a colourful and cultured environment; she was coming to the "bright lights". The reality was different; an industrial background closed and darkened when the sun disappeared. The onset of war then cancelled most regular fun-filled activities.

The club they ran was yards from a central railway hub with the attendant dirty smoggy atmosphere and day-long noise, so the family were glad to put the gloomy location behind them, happy to move to Marple for a quiet country life.

There was no dramatic exodus from the club. It naturally and slowly wound down; it opened for a few hours in the evening, run by Mabel and patronized by locals. Felicity's waistband was expanding, so she rested most afternoons. Anna and Betsy had firm dates for their move to Marple and received confirmed employment in Stockport. Fate had intervened and cleverly moved them onto a new phase in all their lives.

A removal man drove four quiet women from Ardwick to their new house in Marple, followed by another man stacked with their belongings in the van. After a few miles, they relaxed with delighted glances as they swapped crammed city buildings for lengthy green fields.

Felicity broke the silence. 'We're finally on our way.' The girls squeezed hands and looked with delight at the peaceful Cheshire countryside.

When they arrived at Mabel's country home, the girls distributed their treasured boxes in their allotted rooms with jubilation. Now quite large and weary from her pregnancy, Felicity said, 'Just put them in the rooms; we have plenty of time to sort them out.'

The girls were tired but joyful when they retired to bed. This place was where they all wanted to be; it felt right.

World War II rumbled in the background, but the codename Operation Overlord started suddenly in the early hours of 6 June 1944 (D-day). The 1,200-plane airborne raid preceded one of the most significant amphibious military assaults in history involving more than 5,000 vessels. The English Channel was crossed, and approximately 156,000 American, British and Canadian forces landed on five Normandy beaches that day. More than two million Allied troops were in France by the end of August. It resulted in a successful Allied liberation of Western Europe from Nazi Germany's control.

During this momentous time, there were also happenings miles away in Marple. Felicity was not taking over the club, so they were ready to sell it and contacted a few estate agents for assessments. Felicity joined Mabel for moral support. She looked at the interior with fresh eyes, noted the hand-painted, mismatched furniture and homemade chair covers, and laughed. The smell of stale cigarettes and beer was slowly fading. The agents had only one word of interest for the property: 'Location'.

From their enthusiastic photography and measuring, Mabel realised her initial thoughts on the potential of the building were right. The Big Band era was over, focusing on small groups and intimate venues with classy and expensive decor. The club was within the hub of all the local transport and within walking distance of the central hotels; it would be a viable project for someone to develop this site.

After the evaluations, Mabel said to Felicity, 'With my pension and money from the sale, we'll both be quite comfortably off.'

Felicity said, 'Right. That's it; we'll close right now. We need a sign.' She found a large piece of cardboard and a pen and wrote "CLOSED" in big letters, and beneath, "FOR SALE" and Mabel's telephone number.

With linked arms and grinning, Mabel helped the waddling Felicity to the nearby station. They couldn't wait to get home and tell the girls their news.

Marple had unlimited parking so the girls bought an old cheap car, and their friends taught them how to drive. Although it was unnecessary for Felicity to drive, it would give her and Mabel independence. On the first attempt, she passed her test. The examiner looked pointedly at her colossal bump. 'You're not planning to take yourself to the hospital, are you?' he joked.

Felicity laughed, 'Relax! I'm thinking of having a home delivery with three honorary nurses and a midwife in charge.'

He mopped his brow in mock relief. 'In that case, I wish you all the best.'

Mabel luxuriated in her newfound freedom. For the first time in her life, she had three willing drivers to drop her at church functions, take her shopping, and enjoy family drives into the countryside.

Felicity said, 'Take that smug look off your face. You're not retiring. With my newborn, a puppy and two young ladies around the house, there'll be no time for you to put your feet up.'

For Mabel, growing up as an inner-city child, the wonders of living in the countryside were unexpected at her age. The tranquillity and the change of seasons delighted her, and she enjoyed the variety of colourful flowers. She hadn't a clue about their botanical names and vowed to look through Felicity's copious country garden books.

Anna and Betsy had already started their new chapters. It wasn't long before the usual succession of new boyfriends appeared. They looked forward to ballroom dancing in winter, and Snowdonia and the coast were within cycling distance for a day's outing in the summer.

The pregnancy time dragged on for Felicity. The kicking inside was vigorous, 'This is a real footballer. It could be a boy. Would he be dark like his father or pale like me?' The girls stayed quiet while they listened to their mother's bump, hoping to hear something, signalling the sounds of a new life. There was undoubtedly a swishing and gurgling.

On 15th July, an involuntary surge of movement across Felicity's lower abdomen woke her. She noted the time in her bedside notebook. *"First pang 6.00 a.m."* '*It's too early to muster the troops; let them rest. It might be a false alarm. I'll lie back; the other two took hours. Thank God, it's the end of carrying this great thumping weight. It must be ready to nosedive into the real world. Come on, baby!'*

She waited for the next contraction. '*I've no option but to have the girls here watching. It's Saturday morning, and they're not at work.*' Another pang at 6.45 a.m. was duly noted.

'*This is a positive sign. Should the girls be here? I'll have to be brave, with no noise, no histrionics. They mustn't be given the idea that it's an unbearable ordeal and put them off having babies. If the going gets rough, I'll concentrate on Bruno. I really wish he was here to see this.*'

Another couple of contractions followed close together, so Felicity got up, knocked on Mabel's door, and opened it slightly. 'The baby's coming.' Mabel threw back the covers and walked Felicity back to her bedroom. She then bustled downstairs and telephoned Julie, the midwife. The girls, awakened by all the early morning kerfuffle, were determined to behave responsibly and started making breakfast.

Felicity's bedroom became a hub of excitement tinged with trepidation. The girls volunteered to take turns giving their mother back massages whenever she stopped slowly walking around. The midwife waved them away so Felicity could lie down and rest.

Both girls crept back after an hour, and Betsy periodically dabbed her mother's forehead, and Anna sat on the dressing table stool. By mid-morning, the midwife checked progress and said, 'Girls, bring me a bowl of warm water. Felicity, don't push until I say. Just pant now, puff, puff, puff. OK, you can push now. Goodness, this child is in a hurry. One more enormous push. PUSH.'

Mabel held Felicity's sweaty hand as a dark-haired head appeared between her legs. Without further encouragement, the slimy body slid onto the towel, and Julie cut and tied the umbilical cord.

She scooped up the baby, slapped it to make it cry, and wrapped it in a clean towel. 'Well done. He's got a great set of lungs.'

Felicity choked on her dry throat as she mumbled, 'I've got a boy.'

Julie smiled, 'Yes. Let me weigh him and check him over. Mabel, why don't you settle the mother? You girls can put the kettle on and tidy up, please.'

Mabel looked over at the baby's shock of dark hair and slightly olive skin; her lips trembled as she noticed the resemblance to Bruno.

Betsy announced from the back of the room, 'We have a brother.' The girls laughed and cried with mixed heightened emotions and hugged each other, knowing that this episode would stay a bond with them for the rest of their lives.

The beaming smile from their mother confirmed that she felt alright. Felicity's gaze swept the room through the tears of joy and relief. All eyes trained on her, waiting for some profound words.

'I'm dying for a cup of tea,' was all she could muster with her remaining strength.

Julie wrapped the baby in a soft blanket and gently placed him in Felicity's arms. 'Here's your perfect bouncing boy. What will you call him?'

A chorus of 'Carlo' made her chuckle.

Felicity wanted to add another particular Italian name, and he became Carlo Ponti Rowlands, soon shortened to Carl.

Mabel had readily adjusted to a relaxed mode of country life, taking several daily walks with Amber, their new Cavalier King Charles spaniel.

Chapter 22

A few months later, Mabel was sweeping the path when the harsh slamming of car doors startled her. She looked up as two men approached slowly with heavy footsteps.

'Good morning. Do you remember us, Miss Evans? We came into the club.' She certainly did; they were Home Office who came seeking Bruno.

She nodded. Their grim expressions foretold terrible news. She thought, *'Go away. I don't want any sadness to spoil my day. We've had months of tranquillity.'*

They ignored her silence and pressed on with their report. 'We have some news about Lieutenant Bruno Ponti.'

Mabel beckoned the officers into the house and pointed to chairs. Her stomach churned with dread. 'Will this take long? Can I get you a drink?'

They both declined. Detective Watts said, 'I know you'll want the full details. The sergeant at the police station told us this. The Council cleared bomb debris from a stretch of land next to the Exchange Railway Station on the Salford side of the River Irwell. An architect and surveyor measuring for a new building saw a flash of metal sticking up proudly in the ground. The surveyor pulled at it and noticed the iron strip had heavily embossed numbers. He put it in his pocket and said, *"Fancy this surviving the blast? It might be something important. I'll drop it into the Police on my way home."* One old copper had an idea what it was. An identity tag, possibly the army. He asked around the stations to see if it meant anything to anyone.'

Mabel's heart sank as she heard the words 'blast' and 'identity tag', and she stared ahead, wondering how Felicity would take this news.

The detective said, 'The American Army claimed and formally identified it from the number. They said it belonged to Lieutenant Bruno Ponti, who disappeared into thin air months ago. Poor soul, he didn't even make it to the D-Day landings. We handled the initial search and are contacting interested parties over here.'

Mabel heard rustling from the kitchen door and saw Felicity standing with the baby. She had heard everything and stumbled towards the table. Mabel took Carl from her and placed him in his cot. Felicity stared into space, white-faced.

The detective looked at the photo pinned to his file's cover and peered over at the tiny living replica in the cot.

As tears rose and her throat tightened, Felicity said, 'You were right, Mabel; he didn't contact us because he couldn't.'

At the mention of an identity tag, Felicity's stomach lurched as her mind snapped to when Bruno told her the purpose of the dog tag notches. *'I'd never been so horrified to hear the gruesome details of battlefield death. Thank God it didn't happen to him.'*

The men glanced with commiseration at the two sorrowful ladies. Dealing with the tragedy and heartbreak they delivered was always an ordeal. They strode to their car without looking back and drove away wearing the same silent, grim faces.

Mabel said, 'We can now stop hoping he'll turn up. I'm grateful those men were kind enough to bring us the news.'

She hugged Felicity, 'His last words, and I'll never forget them, were, "Take care of Felicity for me." Clearly shown on his face were the depths of love and desolation at leaving you, certainly not the action of a fly-by-night.'

After such unexpected news, large glasses of sherry returned colour to their ashen faces.

Mabel glanced at the clock. 'Anna and Betsy will be here soon. They'll be sad, but at least we know you were not just abandoned. It seems like he was killed only hours after our farewell dinner.'

The finality of the word 'killed' hit Felicity, who let out a piercing scream, 'Nooooo!' and ran, wailing, to her bedroom.

Mabel put the kettle on. She could have kicked herself for choosing such an emotive word.

Felicity lay on her bed, sobbing. This second Home Office visit had pricked the balloon of make-believe. *'He hadn't deserted me, he's been bombed to smithereens, and only that stupid dog tag survived.'*

Days after the initial gut-wrenching shock, she hoped that in time, the cruelty of his death would percolate into a beautiful, happy memory and erase those misplaced thoughts of his betrayal that inveigled her mind for months.

After receiving the devastating news that floored their mother, the girls thought it appropriate to hold a small family ceremony in the garden. Without a formal funeral, this may fill the void for them and bring closure to her. Apart from Mabel, Anna, and Betsy, no one else had met him.

Felicity bought a white rose bush to remember Bruno and his tale of the red and white roses in the vineyard. Felicity's tears ran non-stop as she read the label, 'Au revoir. Until we meet again,' and bent down to plant it in the hole beside the wooden bench. The girls produced a posy of white carnations cut from the garden, tied with a pink ribbon, and handed it to their bereft mother.

Mabel thought it resembled a bridal posy, and to cover her extreme sadness, she whisked Carl out of his pram, scurried into the house and plopped him in the high chair for his lunch.

Felicity grasped the flowers in one hand and tried to keep down the tightening lump in her throat. Betsy felt for her mother's free hand as Anna read aloud an uplifting poem, and they quietly recited The Lord's Prayer. The gathering was sad but informal and light-hearted because the girls hardly knew him. It all felt unreal to them, like play-acting.

On the garden bench, Felicity sat alone, *'I had daydreams tucked away that he would return, and we would continue our life together. A piece of metal found on a bomb site destroyed these. He'd assured me they'd not posted him to a danger zone, which is ironic as he perished on my home soil, only miles away.'*

She had no deep-seated grief as they had only spent one week closely together. However, she keenly felt the loss of a dream life that had been dangled before her and cruelly snatched away.

Mabel returned to bring her indoors. Felicity looked up and held out her hands for comfort as terrible sobs shook her, and she cried piteously, 'I haven't even got a photograph to show Carl what his father looked like. I'm worried he'll fade from my memory.'

'Sadly, the girls and I didn't know him well enough,' said Mabel. 'We can't help you by reminiscing about him or sharing your sorrow, no matter how much we wish to help.'

Felicity stood at the kitchen sink and splashed her face with cold water to wash away the vestiges of tears. It eased the shock of the utter finality of knowing Bruno was dead. *'Another emotional upheaval in this terrible year. I didn't expect things to get any worse, but it has!'*

She was ready to soldier on in sadness alone. *'Mabel was right; Bruno's death has changed nothing for them. They have only experienced good times recently; new jobs introduced exciting friends, a safe, comfortable home environment, and I've given them a surprise bonus, a stepbrother.'*

Mabel interrupted her musings by calling the girls for a sandwich lunch. Felicity wasn't hungry, excused herself and arranged the posy in a glass vase in her bedroom. *'It is a tender enough tribute to mark the short but poignant time I'd known that gentle and kind soul.'* Her heart still ached for Bruno, and as she quietly wept for her loss again, she mourned that he never knew he had a beautiful son.

Later, Mabel suggested they spend the afternoon in the garden, as it was such a warm day. Felicity rested on the bench against the wall. It had been the backdrop for many dramas since they came here. As she sipped a warm tea, she thought of Bruno and tried to remember every detail of their week together. A bizarre memory returned: *'Whatever happened to the nighties and slippers?'*

She heard Mabel's laugh, which jolted her from her recollections. Shocked, she realised they had a bond. Both suffered the promise of a lifelong relationship, blown away by war before it truly began. 'Like Mabel, I must carry on, even though the aching sorrow is still there. Will it always be around?' Grief now had a basis and replaced the uncertainty. She now believed he loved her, but never had the chance to prove it.

Too stricken to weep more, she assumed a pleasant expression and joined the girls. But Mabel knew the strength it took and mentally applauded the bravery of her niece.

A few days after the small ceremony, Felicity's face assumed serenity when she saw her mirror reflection, in contrast to her mind's turmoil.

Mabel enjoyed having an extended family during her retirement. She would have been happy with just the three of them, but the bonus of Carl's baby stages was pure delight.

Sadly but proudly, they could, in all honesty, now state to the child, 'Your father was an American officer, killed in the Second World War.'

Chapter 23

The Government designated the 8th of May 1945 VE Day, 'Victory in Europe'. In a singular action, they cut the streets off from traffic to facilitate the street party celebrations.

The small towns and villages commandeered sports fields and village greens. Food rationing continued, but an array of delicious homemade offerings and a selection of drinks appeared on the long trestle tables. Many people kept cake, pie ingredients, and sandwich fillers, guessing this celebration was not far away.

In Marple, they used the field adjoining the church, and in mid-morning, Mabel and Betsy went to help with the preparations. Anna and Frank, her steady boyfriend, would visit other festivities in the area to greet their friends. They joined in the dancing and singing, music provided by the BBC, local musicians and even wind-up gramophones.

Felicity used Carl as a reason to stay home. The family didn't press her to go out; it was too soon after the terrible news about Bruno. She was not quite ready to join in the fun and felt consoled by the gift of his precious child. Next year will be better, she assured herself.

It was easy for Felicity to mingle with the many war widows. Betsy and Anna were proud of their baby brother and not embarrassed when they explained, 'His father was an American officer, killed in the war.' They told any new friends that their parents were divorced and their father still lived in Crewe, which pigeonholed them neatly.

Ardwick Green seemed like another world. Was it only five years? Life had moved into another dimension. During the past year, they moved house; a baby was born. Anna now had a car and a steady boyfriend, Frank. Betsy had a gaggle of girlfriends and, with them, experimented with the latest makeup and hairstyles.

Grateful for the tranquillity, Mabel and Felicity sat out in the weak spring sunshine and watched Carlo crawling on the lawn, experiencing his first touch of grass. Mabel, transfixed with the succession of different daffodils, picked one and sniffed it. 'These are scented!'

'Yes, a lovely bonus with those frilly ones.'

'Anna's on a winner with Frank; he's so calm and pleasant. I'm not sure where he works. Did he say he's a car mechanic?'

'His garage relocated to Stockport six years ago, something to do with high-end car sales and maintenance. He lodges with a local family to save money, so it might be an engagement ring he buys next. Here they come! They look excited, don't put the kettle on yet.'

The couple approached the garden bench, hand in hand. The sun backlit Anna's auburn hair into a bronze halo. Animated, they spoke simultaneously, then stopped, looked at each other and started again. Frank waved to Anna to go ahead with the announcement.

'We were just about to announce our engagement when Mr Timpson offered me the job of starting a branch in Birmingham. They are going to specialise in large tents and marquees for functions.' Breathless, she sat down and clasped her mother's hand.

Frank said, 'My family live there, so accommodation and work won't be a problem.'

Betsy shrieked and hugged both of them, joined by their mother and great-aunt. Amber ran from one to another in bewilderment at the laughing and crying. Little Carlo toddled over, covered in soil, and dusted with daffodil pollen. His plaintive cry brought them down to earth.

The happy couple drove to the local church to see Reverend Collins. It was a Norman building topping a hill, and the dark vestry smelt of musty hymn books, which vied with the scent of newly arranged flowers ready to decorate the church. They liaised with the cleric and chose a Saturday afternoon suitable for their nuptials. The Reverend asked, 'How many guests will attend the service?'

Anna said, 'I don't know, as the invitations haven't been sent out. As soon as I have some idea, I'll contact you.'

'Have you thought about a reception? Most Saturday venues get booked up months ahead.'

Frank piped up, 'I've got an idea. Why not have an informal reception in your garden, Anna?'

The Reverend nodded his agreement, 'I've seen the transformation of your house, and the garden is a picture. Another helpful tip, the Golden Lion keeps a stock of fold-up chairs for hire. Worth a try.'

The pair hurried to tell the family, fired with enthusiasm. Anna announced, 'We've got the first of June. Mum, Frank thought we could use the garden for the reception. Reverend Collins said the garden was perfect; "It's a picture", were his exact words!'

Felicity glowed with the compliment, 'Great idea. That just leaves the food. We'll sort something out.'

Wedding preparations started in earnest. Anna and Betsy shopped in Manchester for invitations and white shoes and were surprised at the high quality and variety of the cards. One chosen pack was warm and suitably worded for family and close friends; the other was a plain card with spaces for remarks. Both had silver deckle edges, scattered with horseshoes and orange blossom. Even though mass-produced, viewed singly, they appeared very attractive.

Then they tried on plain white court shoes with detachable bows for everyday wear, leaving only dress material for the wedding and bridesmaid to be found.

Manchester was founded in the Victorian days and became the centre of the cotton trade, concentrating on manufacturing and garment production for worldwide consumption. Huge mills, warehouses and homes for the workers were necessary; more significant, opulent houses were built for mill owners on the outskirts. Commerce needed large shopping areas to exhibit their wares. The building exteriors were softened by decorative wrought iron railings, an interlacing of lines suggestive of Gothic tracery.

Anna and Betsy were not interested in architecture but focussed on fine cotton lawn for the bridal dress, not the usual opulent satin. They deemed it more suitable for a village wedding, attended by countryfolk with a garden setting for the reception.

Later at home, the cards were spread out and placed with the compiled lists of recipients. To their surprise, Anna suggested Frank write the cards in his ornate copperplate handwriting using his gold fountain pen. 'Who thought a mechanic would be so artistic?'

He dismissed the praise with a light wave. 'I learnt during free evening classes in junior school in the holidays. Some lads were shown how to make paper flowers.'

Anna said, 'He never fails to amaze me!'

They posted the invitations and awaited replies. It was fun to open them together in the evenings; their celebrations started long before the wedding day.

Anna had her mother's acceptance of the tricky situation and had telephoned her father to ask if he would give her away at the ceremony. He accepted readily and said, 'It will thrill your Gran to bits to receive an invitation, and she will certainly enjoy buying a new outfit.' He was spot on. Delighted and proud to attend, Ethel bought an acceptance card and wrote it in her best handwriting and sent it by return post.

'I am delighted to accept and pleased there are only three weeks to wait until your joyous occasion. I look forward to catching up with the family. A lot has happened to everyone.'

Mabel had volunteered to organise the alcohol and soft drink orders and, sensibly, a tarp in case of rain.

The following day, Felicity entered the local confectioners for fresh bread and admired a gateau on a side table. Mrs West, the owner, told her it was a party order. Felicity had an idea, 'Do you cater for functions?'

Mrs West nodded. 'We get the smaller enquiries. The usual sandwiches, but we've done nothing else for a while. What have you got in mind?'

'My daughter, Anna, is getting married and wants to hold an informal reception in the garden. We don't know the numbers yet, but if all the church congregation pop in, it could be possibly a hundred.'

'Let me think about it, and I'll let you know.'

Felicity didn't want her to think about it. No other villager could do it, and she slyly added, 'Your small pies, sausage rolls and individual fancy cakes are lovely, perfect finger food.'

Pleased with the flattery, Mrs West nodded, 'In which case, I'm game. I'll treat it as a trial run, and if successful, it might be worth adding to our business.'

She heaved a sigh of relief. 'Thank you so much. I'll get you the numbers. If you provide the nosh, we'll do the rest. It's not a champagne and caviar do, nothing too posh, just make a lot.'

Mrs West looked pleased with the prospect of a lovely little earner.

Felicity said, 'It's your good deed for Anna. We couldn't hope to get a caterer at such short notice. Can you see me doing it? They'd get cheese and crackers if they're lucky.'

Mrs West laughed. Felicity continued, eager to complete the deal. 'I'll pop in to see how you are progressing. Don't worry about the budget; I've saved on not hiring a hall, so I can afford to be more extravagant on the food.'

'I've always liked your Anna. She's a lovely girl, so polite.'

'When I tell her, she'll be in to see you like a shot. It's all a bit rushed because they'll take new jobs in Birmingham immediately after the wedding.'

Chapter 24

The organist, Miss Davies, sat relaxed and ready at the organ and responded to the vicar's nod by striking the rousing chords of Mendelsohn's Bridal March, the signal for the bride to walk down the aisle on her father's arm.

A borrowed circlet of filigree topped Anna's simple white cotton floor-length dress trimmed with blue, highlighting her coppery hair. A posy of flowers with flowing blue ribbons completed her outfit.

Just behind her, the bridesmaid, Betsy, wore a long floral cotton dress, a posy and a blue ribbon bow perched cheekily on top of her blonde hair. Her face glowed with excitement.

Anna looked around with pride at the posh occasion dresses by older relatives. Her mother was elegant in a pale blue sheath with a navy hat, and her great aunt Mabel was in a teal green satin suit. Her grandmother, Ethel, looked smart in a silver-grey dress and jacket ensemble topped with a cerise hat with feathers sticking up at frightening angles.

George kept his composure and looked smart in his best grey suit, grateful for the chance to make it up to the girls for the upheaval in their lives. He had previously offered funds to help with the wedding, but they were funding it themselves, being a modern couple.

Jenny, holding Carl's hand, looked in wonderment at this gathering. They didn't know or probably didn't care to be grossly overdressed on such a simple occasion. They felt special today, like the royalty they were. Jenny smiled at them fondly as she and her sister led Carl to a seat at the back.

The minister wore a newly pressed black robe with a white sash for the Christian wedding ceremony and savoured a moment of complete silence. He scanned the merry groups of guests; many had been parishioners under his pastoral care. Today, in front of his loving community, he felt like a natural teacher, living part of the

Bible. He loudly announced the favoured Palm Sunday hymn, 'All Glory Laud and Honour,' when he remembered where he was. The first dramatic bars echoed around the church and signalled the congregation to stand. They sang with great gusto from the hymn books.

When seated, the minister changed his mind and gave a brief address, abandoning the long sermon he had rehearsed. This family gathering did not need pomp and oration; it was a cause for celebration, not words. He gave God's blessings on the couple and their marriage.

'We are happy to welcome Frank into our midst. He's joining a small family that has positively affected the village in the short time they have been here. They have embraced country life enthusiastically after their years in the city. It made us look at the beauty surrounding us with fresh eyes. We are honoured to be included in this wonderful family wedding celebration.'

The children were unusually peaceful, told something nice was happening. The married couple held hands and walked down the aisle and into the warm sun rays outside, where the excited children threw handfuls of rice and rose petals.

They had invited everyone in the church to Mabel's house for the reception. Some fancied the short walk, while a villager with a car offered to make a few journeys for the less mobile.

At the house, the reception finger buffet on hired trestle tables awaited. The table was covered in garlands of garden flowers, disguising the white sheets used as tablecloths.

Neighbours and those not officially invited to the wedding ceremony dropped in to congratulate the happy couple. They stayed more than a minute when shown the tempting buffet.

Mrs West had pushed the boat out. Everything was miniature; tiny pork pies, chicken and beef triangular sandwiches with suitable dressings. As a joke, Mabel added, 'Don't forget the caviar.' Crab tarts garnished with tiny black beads, probably tinned, called her bluff. She resisted spiriting them away for herself, but it proved a talking point.

Jenny was now a successful businesswoman and drove a new car. Helping establish the club set her on the path to owning her own administration business. She and her sister offered George and Ethel a ride afterwards to Manchester's central station. She assured Mabel, 'It is no trouble. It will prolong the day and help us get acquainted.' She and her sister had taken complete charge of Carl for the afternoon. It was time for them to relax and socialise. They said to Mabel, 'It's been a labour of love. We volunteer for babysitting anytime; he is so well-behaved.'

'That angelic demeanour will go when he starts nursery and gets away from adults,' Mabel replied. 'You'd better prepare yourselves for a monster,' she warned.

Three avuncular figures, Syd, Bill and Charlie, Mabel's old friends, who'd travelled from Manchester and arrived wearing old straw hats, gave the proceedings a musical comedy air. They entered into the day's spirit and gave out drinks with much merriment and banter.

The girls showed George and Ethel around the house and then the garden. Since the invitation, they had established a closer relationship and would probably visit each other more frequently, forming a warmer rapport after the long absence.

They had not visited Marple, and Felicity had not returned to Crewe, so it was a fitting occasion for a reunion. Anna had previously told them about their mother's surprise baby. When they met Carl, a feeling of warmth towards a new family member surprised them; although not related by blood, they somehow felt like close relatives.

It delighted Anna to see her parents chatting amiably together about the garden, an extra joy on her wedding day. He told her he was retiring early, playing bowls and helping run the railway club, where he now had a few female admirers. Gone was the taciturn husband Felicity remembered. She had only really known him doing hard manual work, tired from long hours and no doubt under some stress having to provide for the family.

Ethel now walked with a stick but was lively and proud to be asked to bake homemade cakes for the bazaars and church functions. The reunion was healing as they had all changed and moved on. They remained friends with shared history, genuinely pleased to be reunited.

The three 'uncles', Syd, Bill and Charlie, already part of the extended family, engaged themselves in tidying up and restoring the garden furniture to their usual places, dotted around the paths and borders. They stacked the hired chairs within the accessible pickup area near the garden gate.

Mabel had pressed them to take a few leftover crates of ale as they piled into Bill's van and set off for Manchester, pleased with themselves and the welcome parting gifts.

Before the newlyweds left for Frank's apartment to pack for Birmingham, they threw off their shoes and sank into the easy chairs. Betsy and Felicity joined them, grateful for a cup of Mabel's real ground coffee served from her giant pot. They went over the day's success, and funny antics, who wore what, what was said and when. One of Frank's friends had a camera and was engaged as their unofficial photographer. They promised to come over and reminisce once more when the pictures were developed.

The family waved Frank and Anna off from the front doorway. Felicity said, 'I expected to feel sad, but I'm not. They are so perfect together, both energetic and forceful. They will make a formidable team in Birmingham. She's so happy, and I look forward to watching their progress. What an amazing day; it was just perfect.'

Chapter 25

Bruno's Italian family lived within their vineyard estate in Napa, California. His father, Carlo Ponti, came in from the winery office looking hangdog and chastened. His small stature was not usually evident, because his noisy enthusiasm made him larger than life. He slumped in a chair and his wife, Eva, became alarmed at his sudden lack of drive. He had recently retired to let Tony and Franco, their two sons, run the winery. Franco was now the manager, while Tony was office-based as the financial expert.

Each of his sons differed from the other, and he often wondered from which side of the family they inherited their genes. Tony was short and stubby and had slicked-back dark hair with a side parting, and the comb lines showed he was an obvious user of hair pomade. Franco was taller with a widow's peak and a clipped pencil moustache.

'Is there something wrong with the business?' Eva inquired.

'Nothing to be alarmed about. That's not what's wrong; it's running like clockwork.' They both saw the funny side of this ridiculous remark and laughed uproariously.

It was good to hear them laughing again after the previous worrying and sad months. Carlo was happy to see Eva smile, even fleetingly. The rest of the family had reluctantly accepted Bruno's death as a tragic casualty of war and carried on as usual. It was comforting to relive Bruno's memorial and remember the considerable turnout.

Eva said, 'It amazed me how fast the news of Bruno's death spread through the community. We didn't realise how highly they regarded him. He was a prime example of the homegrown talent that returned to enrich our business, but sadly, he didn't come back this time.'

The community had lost a popular member, and their grief was genuine. The presiding minister said, 'We have a powerful reminder that war is not a game. When the first casualty is a prominent member of one of our founding families, it hits us all forcibly. His is a sacrifice not one of us wanted or expected to pay.'

Carlo said, 'I remember the crowds spilling out of the church onto the surrounding approaches. The hounding press with cameras and microphones was too much for me. I wanted to run and hide; I'm glad I'm not a film star.'

'Tony presented me with Bruno's dog tag the day before. I remember his words well. *"We have only this as a lasting, tangible token. It must be yours to keep and hold tightly on your black days, to remind you he loved you deeply."* He held back tears until the end of the sentence but couldn't help himself. I well up just thinking of him. He was right; I clutched the tag to give me bravery through the service.'

'Let me have a look at it. I wonder where they got the idea of having it dipped in gold and found a nice chain?'

'He told me he showed it to a jeweller friend who had seen medals and memorabilia items treated this way. It's a thin gold plating on the dog tag to keep the numbers clear, and you can change the chain so it will never become unfashionable.'

'It's not an everyday necklace, but nice to have it.'

'I like that they provided a delicate wooden stand, so it's not just stuck in a box.' She fondly traced the raised numbers with her fingertips before looping it over her neck.

Over dinner, Carlo looked fondly at his wife. Her dark warm brown eyes had saddened again. She was round and cuddly, hugging everyone at the slightest excuse, making them feel loved and included in her affections. He said, 'I thought we would feel at peace when we knew what had happened to Bruno, but we're still unsettled.'

Eva nodded. 'Perhaps if we went over to see where he died, it might help?'

Carlo jumped to his feet. 'You're right! I'm not needed here for a few days. I think passenger planes are flying into England now. We will go as soon as we get our visas.' He grabbed her hand and rushed her into the office to contact the travel agent and plan the trip. 'Thank goodness Bruno sent us the Cavallo's address as soon as he found them. How long is it since we saw them? It must be over thirty years. We are so old, cara.'

It was a momentary diversion, and as she broke away from his cuddle, she said with a brave smile, 'It might give us some closure. I'm off to decide on my packing.' Strength replaced the weariness and apathy in her voice; she had a purpose, something on which to focus.

The war was over. The returning servicemen had adapted to the easy air travel from the States to Europe and looked forward to revisiting places of interest. A global shake-up occurred; millions of people's lives had changed.

Wartime showed everyone other ways of living, which altered their attitudes. Relaxed access to food varieties replaced die-hard culinary habits, and department stores transformed shopping. Women no longer felt tied to the house; they had work and money in their pockets for the first time.

Divorces were plentiful as the soldiers returned to their wives, changed over the years with different expectations. Many independent women saw an exciting future for themselves and their children; they rejected the past and, sadly, sometimes the men in it.

Tony and Franco were relieved to see a lighter mood change in their parents as they left for San Francisco's international airport. They were excited, like children setting off on a picnic. It was pleasing to see them enthusiastic again. Crossing the Atlantic by air was a novelty. Carlo said to Eva, 'We were lucky to emigrate from the U.K. on one of the new steam liners. Do you remember, it took days?'

The Ponti's arrived in Manchester; after a long but easy flight and a train ride up from London, they caught a cab and went straight to their hotel near Piccadilly in the city centre.

After a day of rest and adjustment to English time, they rang their friends, Ricardo and Lena. Bruno had given his parents their contact details. Carlo rang them to tell them they'd arrived safely and said they would drop by the cafe after picking up their rented car the following day.

Their next priority was to contact Detectives Watts and Jenkins and arrange a visit to the site near Exchange Station.

Detective Watts was available that afternoon. He picked them up in a police car and drove the few minutes to the area flattened by the bomb. It was now a building construction site enclosed with hoarding.

Eva's hands shook in the car, and she felt queasy, but when confronted with a hive of city industry, it disappeared. Carlo was stiff in his resolve to remain calm for his wife's sake.

Some foundations were ready for the building to start. Architects with sheaves of plans were kings surveying their domain. Groups of engineers dressed in hard hats assumed control; the bulldozers were leaving, and cement mixers replaced them.

They were two smartly dressed tourists who aroused a couple of curious glances, making them feel superfluous in all this industry.

'I'm glad we came,' Eva said to Carlo, 'But there's nothing here for us.'

'Yes,' Carlo said, agreeing that this new modern building couldn't be a shrine. 'It was worth coming here; perhaps we can now treat this as our sentimental journey instead.'

Eva took his hand after they declined a lift to the hotel. They strolled away from the area without looking back and ambled back to the main road. Lunch was taken at The Old King's Arms, one of the remaining black and white Tudor buildings in the Old Shambles, dating back to Shakespearian days.

Manchester Cathedral was next on their list. It looked smaller and darker than they remembered. The afternoon jogged memories of their brief stay there, sandwiched between Italy and America. They continued their trip down memory lane and caught a bus. Now the war was over, the powerful council could carry on with the slum clearance and include recent bomb damage.

After the First World War and the recession in Italy, England and America invited Italian workers to replace the many war casualties. Carlo's parents accepted the challenge and started work in Manchester, but they desperately felt the cold and dampness in winter and looked further afield for opportunities. They chose California when they heard the climate was warmer than the U.K. There were work prospects in new vineyards which suited their expertise and a chance to join other expatriates.

Carlo said, 'I'm glad we're in Napa. It was a hard slog at first, real back-breaking work on the land. We worked hard to restore those dilapidated buildings and bring the struggling vines to life.

'Your Pa had the vision; he was a real pioneer; he would be proud if he could see how it's developed today.'

He missed his parents and quickly changed the subject. 'I'm looking forward to seeing the Cavallo's tomorrow. Bruno wrote they were well and happy. Is it really forty-odd years since we last saw them? I can't believe it.'

After a sentimental day, they were ready to change their focus from a sad pilgrimage to a joyous reunion. The following day, they drove to Stockport to visit Lena and Ricardo. The cafe was easy to find, and they parked nearby. Overjoyed in each other's company, they told many fresh stories to blend with their memories. The meeting, tinged with sadness, was fraught with emotion.

The Cavallo's enjoyed Manchester's city life and catering. They worked hard and were profitable, so they didn't move away to Stockport until nearing retirement. Ricardo asked Carlo, 'How's Felicity? No doubt devastated to hear of Bruno's death?'

Carlo looked puzzled, shook his head, and looked at Eva questioningly.

Eva looked mystified. 'Who's Felicity?'

Ricardo said, 'Ah! You didn't know about her. We met when Bruno gave us your address. She's lovely, about his age, and although they'd just met, they seemed besotted with each other. I think it was love at first sight for both of them. They were not youngsters, and it seemed serious. We felt privileged to enjoy the company of such a sweet, romantic couple.'

Eva and Carlo stared at each other in disbelief.

'Fancy that,' said Carlo. 'Our Bruno being so infatuated at last.'

Lena said, 'He must have been planning something. He took me aside and asked about diamond rings and whether Felicity looked like a girl who would prefer a solitaire. I assured him that any woman would love a sizeable solitaire. He laughed when I emphasised the word "large".'

Eva smiled at the lack of subtlety in her friend's advice. 'What does this Felicity look like?'

'A blonde, straight hair, grey eyes, small features. Very pretty and vivacious, especially when explaining something. We could understand what the attraction was.'

'Do you know her surname and her address?'

'No, I'm sorry, we didn't ask. But she came from Crewe with two teenage daughters.'

Carlo once again invited their friends to visit them in California, and they promised to keep in touch. On the way to the hotel, Eva asked, 'How can we possibly find her?'

He shrugged. 'We can certainly try. I'll ask the detective and see what he says.'

Eva was happy and eager. 'Can we do it today?'

'Yes! We'll make a call as soon as we return to our hotel room. O.K., calm down, Honey.'

It heartened them to imagine that Bruno's last days were loving and full of happiness. They had to find Felicity, who, according to Lena, was something special to him.

Within minutes of reaching their hotel room, the operator put Carlo through to Detective Watts.

Chapter 26

The toddler, Carl, pulled himself around the cottage living room, holding on to the furniture while Mabel stood guard, encouraging him, ready with a steadying hand. She glanced through the window as a long limousine drew up outside the gate. *'This looks interesting,'* she thought, putting the lad into his cot in the nursery for his afternoon nap.

A well-dressed couple looked around slowly at the garden as they approached the front door. The gentleman pointed to the colourful hollyhocks anchored to canes with string. Mabel immediately knew they weren't local, possibly foreigners, by their pale expensive travel wear. The lady clutched a small cream leather handbag. She reckoned they were in their early seventies, both short and stocky with dark grey hair and swarthy skin. She had visions of them as a retired, married Mediterranean couple.

His American drawl came as a surprise. 'Sorry to disturb you, Ma-am, I'm looking for Miss Mabel Evans?' She opened the door wider to get a better view and to welcome them.

'I'm Mabel. Can I help you?' Intrigued, she wondered why Americans were looking for her. Then the penny dropped.

Carlo held out his hand and introduced himself. 'I'm Carlo Ponti, and this is my wife, Eva. We're on vacation from the States.'

Suddenly Mabel felt apprehensive. This was no casual drop-in; these were Bruno's parents. They seemed a pleasant enough couple, but she didn't want to be churned up with their grief. She'd moved on from the dead to the living.

Mabel stood back and pointed to the living room. 'Do come in.'

Eva stepped over the threshold and smiled warmly at Mabel, 'Thank you for seeing us.' The smell of expensive perfume wafted along the hallway as Mabel followed them.

'Please sit down, and I'll put the kettle on. Would you like tea?

'That would be so kind.' Eva took in the quaint artefacts dotted around the room, trying to fathom how this woman had known Bruno.

Mabel's mind was racing as she made a pot of tea. She grabbed a tray cloth from the kitchen drawer and picked the best bone china from the top shelf. When she returned, Carlo stood up to help her, 'Please, let me put that on the table,' and effortlessly took hold of the laden tray.

She let him, as it seemed a gracious gesture. She was not used to such polite manners after working with youngsters in the pub and club.

The clock showed it was three, and Mabel hoped they might have gone before Felicity returned from shopping and late lunch with Jenny. Felicity had settled into a new regime, and Mabel felt protective of her niece. *'No more sorrow, please'*, she silently begged. *'We've moved on.'*

Mabel poured the tea and looked at Eva, sitting in one of the floral armchairs. 'Do you take milk, Mrs Ponti?' It felt strange using that name after trying so hard to forget it.

'Just a little, please,' she replied. 'This is my husband, Carlo, and please call me Eva. You have a quaint house and garden. I just love English flowers.'

Mabel took out the ironed cotton and lace napkins and made light conversation whilst she placed the cup of tea on the side table. 'Where in the States are you from?'

'Napa, California. We've been here a few days already.'

She wanted to get the main topic out of the way; the small talk was palling. 'It was dreadful to hear of Bruno's disappearance.' She couldn't bring herself to say the word death.

Eva looked down. 'It's the worst news. You never want to hear it again.'

Mabel nodded. 'Those who knew him thought it strange of him to disappear and cause anyone distress. It was not in his character. How did you find me? Did the detectives give you my address?'

Carlo said, 'Yes. We've been visiting old friends in Stockport, and they mentioned a girl who visited them with Bruno. We hoped you might have details about a girlfriend called Felicity?'

'Bruno came to the Club initially to find simple accommodation and told us he wanted to trace this Italian family, the Cavallo's, and we tracked them down.'

'We saw them yesterday. Bruno told Lena he hoped to buy Felicity a ring when he returned on leave. They thought she was a charming lady. Apparently, his decision was sudden, but I suppose that's how wartime is. Now the club's closed, we have no other way to find her. Detective Watts gave us your details as the only locals Bruno had befriended.'

Eva sat looking from one to the other; her dark brown eyes looked haunted, still profoundly affected by her terrible loss.

Mabel realised she could spare Felicity the angst of meeting Bruno's grieving parents. She knew what the Ponti's were after and could quickly get rid of them. They certainly need never find out about the baby. Felicity wouldn't want a claim on Carl or them spiriting him away to another country.

As she studied them, immense compassion overwhelmed her for this sad couple. She looked down into her lap, *'You don't know that we, too, have felt immense grief over your son.'*

Before Mabel had time to say or do anything, in swept Felicity, her arms full of rustling paper bags, all agog, to meet the owners of the impressive car outside.

The Ponti's scanned all the details of her animated face, 'Jenny cut short our shopping expedition, so I've come home early.'

Carlo stood up, and Felicity put her bags down and walked toward him to shake hands. She moved to Eva, who rose from her chair to greet this vivacious lady.

Mabel hurriedly introduced them, freed from the life-changing dilemma she'd faced. She stood back, powerless as the drama unfolded, unable to stop the impact of this historic meeting. 'Felicity, meet Bruno's parents, Eva and Carlo.'

To their astonishment, Mabel added, 'She's my niece, and we live here with her two teenage daughters, Anna and Betsy.'

Felicity's mouth dropped open. 'Why are you here? Have they found him?'

Carlo looked into her eyes. 'I'm so sorry. We don't have any news.'

Mabel saw Felicity's shoulders drop. All anticipation dashed. 'Sit down, and I'll fetch another cup.'

Eva blinked back tears at Felicity's disappointment. *'So, there was something between them.'* She looked directly at her and stated, 'You loved him.'

Felicity nodded. However small, anything that had happened to him was important to them now. Their sunken faces and eyes reflected a loss that seemed beyond their grasp. It reminded her of her suffering, and suppressed tears welled up. These were Bruno's beloved parents, and she instinctively got up and held out her arms to hug Eva, which forged an instant common bond.

Carlo watched this huddle of grief and stood immobile. Mabel positioned the extra China cup and gave out hankies to the women.

Eva had found a connection to her beloved late son. He had loved them, and they continued to love him. He was no longer a painful picture in their minds. Together, by talking, they could bring him to life until time to let go again.

Felicity composed herself enough to enquire about their friends. 'Have you been here long enough to visit the Cavallo's?'

Glad of the diversion, Carlo said, 'Yes, they told us about meeting you, and that's how we came to be here. We're still trying to put all the pieces together.'

Felicity looked over at Mabel; her eyes widened questioningly, and she inclined her head towards the nursery. She desperately needed to know if she'd mentioned Carl.

Mabel shook her head slightly in silent response.

Felicity quickly continued the conversation. 'I enjoyed meeting Lena and Ricardo. How are they? Are they still in Stockport?'

Eva said, 'They are well, thank you. Yes, still in Stockport but recently retired from the cafe. We're hoping they will visit us in Napa. They told us about meeting you but only knew your Christian name.'

The importance of this meeting suddenly swamped Felicity when shouts of 'Mama' from the nursery cut across it and galvanised her into action.

She hurried off and reappeared with her son cradled on her hip. With a spontaneous theatrical gesture, and an outstretched arm pointing to the couple, she looked down and announced to the toddler, 'Carl, meet your grandfather and grandmother.'

Carlo and Eva, like marble statues, sat transfixed with shock; Felicity thought they would never move. Then, many seconds later, it sank in, and absolute joy swept through their bodies.

Carlo asked, 'Is this Bruno's son? We were never told and would have come over from the beginning to help you in any way we could.'

Eva stared open-mouthed at a mini replica of her son, savouring every detail of his little face. Completely confused, she didn't know whether to cry from sheer happiness, losing her son, or exhaustion and shock.

Felicity replied, 'Yes, it's Bruno's. It seems feeble now, but there were so many American servicemen in Britain; I heard over two million passed through. Your troops were here for years, and they labelled G.I. brides as chancers who saw an easy ticket to America. They even chartered a liner for them as there were thousands.'

Eva looked up from the boy. 'G.I. brides? Did you actually marry Bruno?'

Felicity said, 'He vanished before Carl was born; he didn't even know I was expecting. Neither did I until weeks after he'd left. We hadn't married, and I didn't need any help. We'd heard stories that when G.I. brides got over there, they found themselves amongst poorer people who needed help. There were no promised ranches or mansions, and many came home disillusioned.'

Eva accepted the explanation and understood a little better.

Mabel said, 'We were all grief-stricken and had no addresses or contacts. We have a comfortable life here and didn't want to be involved in anything distasteful. We wanted to protect the child.'

Carlo said, 'I must apologise for putting you on the defensive. I just hate to imagine you coping alone.'

Mabel lightened the mood and laughed at this. 'Hardly alone in this setup.'

'How old is he? May I pick him up?' Eva asked, and Felicity brought the toddler over. Eva held herself in check to stop squeezing the little mite to death in a big hug.

Carlo strode over and stroked the toddler's dark hair. He looked down at Eva in disbelief; a radiant smile had transformed his wife.

Felicity said, 'He's thirteen months, and his name is Carlo after you. I thought Bruno would have liked that, but he's known as Carl, which is lucky now you're both together.'

Eva and Carlo were soon on all fours, looking at Carl's latest toy, and their eyes fixed on everything he did. Sorrow and grief melted away.

Eva said to Carl, 'I'm your Nonna,' and looked up to Mabel and Felicity, 'It means grandmother.'

Mabel whispered to Felicity, 'What an incredible afternoon this is turning out to be.'

Eva said, 'I hope I'm not speaking out of turn, but did Bruno get the chance to propose to you?'

'No, why?' Felicity cocked her head.

'When we visited the Cavallo's, they said that Bruno seemed serious about you and discussed buying a ring.'

Felicity smiled, 'That's so kind of you to tell me. I had hoped so. We visited Blackpool for the fun and the atmosphere, and he mentioned it would be nice to spend our honeymoon there. We truly believed we'd spend the rest of our lives together. It wasn't a proposal as such; it was a statement of fact.'

This last sentence brought tears to her eyes, and she bit her lip, trying not to start the churning in her stomach. It was still there, even after all this time.

Eva said, 'We didn't know what we were looking for when we came over. It was just unfinished business, some sort of closure. If we hadn't come to England, we would always have lived in a void. Never did I imagine such a wonderful chapter starting.' She had already made an internal promise, *'He's Bruno's son, and we'll give him enough backing and education to follow his dreams.'*

It didn't take long for Felicity to realise the prospects opening up and lying ahead if she took advantage of being admitted to Bruno's family and industry.

Carlo said, 'Eva's getting carried away. Naturally thrilled. Such a tremendous gift after all the uncertainty and sorrow.' He looked at his grandson and savoured one of the most beautiful, unexpected moments they would treasure forever. Losing Bruno had been unbearable, but a gorgeous new family member uplifted them.

Felicity put her arm around Mabel as they watched the doting grandparents. She whispered, 'If I hadn't got back early, would you have told them?'

Without hesitation, her aunt said, 'Fate decided for me. Though I must admit, I was becoming sympathetic.'

Felicity remembered the holdall stashed upstairs.

'We still have some of Bruno's things, a few photos, but the clothes and shoes are fairly new. Do you want to take them back with you, or shall I give them to the church? If you don't mind, I'd like to keep some photos for Carl.'

Eva looked wistfully through the family photos and handed them back. 'You keep them, as you say; Carl should have something.'

Felicity was only interested in one picture, picked it out, and passed it to Eva, 'Who is this little chappie called Edoardo?' She dared not breathe and waited what seemed a lifetime for a response.

Eva smiled, recognising the little boy in the picture. 'This is Eddie; he starts school next year. Doesn't he look like your Carl here? It's Bruno's nephew, Tony's eldest boy.'

Felicity's whole body relaxed with this news. It wasn't Bruno's child. His brother, Tony, must have given him this photo to remind him of his nephew.

Carlo touched Eva's arm. 'We've got to go, Honey. Dinner's booked for seven-thirty.'

Felicity said, 'I'm sure you'd like to see Carl again before you leave. When do you go back?' Felicity asked.

'Tomorrow. May we come for an hour before leaving for the airport in the morning?'

'Of course, you must come again.'

Carlo hugged Felicity warmly and turned to give Mabel a long handshake, which turned into another hug and a kiss on the cheek. Amber enjoyed a few hard pats on the back as they stood by the front door.

Carlo gave Felicity a pleading look as he dragged Eva away from the house. Felicity picked up Carl, 'Let's see Nonna back to the car.'

The doting new grandparents reluctantly got in. Eva waved goodbye with two hands and lots of mock kisses as they drove away. 'See you tomorrow,' she shouted.

There were no tears; this was not goodbye. For Eva, it was a wonderful beginning.

In the car, Eva was babbling. 'It's unbelievable. Wait until we tell the family back home. It will amaze Lena and Ricardo that we found Felicity and a baby.'

Felicity couldn't hold her tears in, and put Carl down while she hunted in her sleeve for a handkerchief. She stood in the road, stunned, and watched the car as it drove out of sight.

Mabel walked out and escorted them inside, stopping to embrace and comfort her sobbing niece. 'We have no control over the tears of loss and grief, always hovering over us, waiting for the next trigger.'

They sat on the bench against the wall as Carl played outside on the path with his bright red plastic lorry, watched curiously by Amber. Mabel looked sideways at her niece, shocked at the glum face, and tried to cheer her up.

'What's the betting we'll all be in America next week!' Mabel said.

Felicity nodded. 'That's what I'm afraid of. We'll have to be careful.'

The following day, the Ponti's arrived as scheduled. They played with Carl while Felicity made drinks, and they moved to chairs in the garden to enjoy the fresh air and the warmth of the morning sun.

After an hour of pleasantries and playing, Carlo asked Felicity, 'I know this is still a shock, but would you like to come over and bring Carl to the States to meet everyone? Please don't worry about the cost or arrangements; we could organise everything if you let us know a date.'

Felicity looked knowingly at Mabel, who smiled in agreement. 'I'll give it some thought.'

Eva pressed a folded piece of paper into Felicity's hand and tried not to seem too pleading. 'Here are our details in Napa. We're on the telephone now. Please come soon.'

They all walked to the car, and Eva turned to Felicity; stemming the tears and a quivering bottom lip, she said, 'This is for you.'

Felicity looked down at the golden dog tag and chain in her open hand. The gold glinted in the weak sunshine, outlining the embossed number. When she realised what it was, she hastily pushed it back to Eva. 'I can't take this.'

Eva closed Felicity's hand around the tag. 'I have memories and now a beautiful grandson. Why not keep it for Carl if you won't take it?'

The gesture overwhelmed Felicity. It was such a monumental keepsake. She looked down at the token of death and let it swing on its chain. The precious metal was hypnotic but, even transformed, coated in gold; it swept her back to the last time she held it, in bed with Bruno. She shivered, remembering the explanation of the ghoulish details on the battlefields. She thought, *'It's done its duty, but I can never wear it. Such a symbol of finality.'*

Today, it seemed prophetic. One day, she might tell Eva the story, but not now.

'Thank you so much, but why don't we share it?'

Eva agreed as they hugged. She was more reluctant to leave than ever. Everyone knew that if she could have stolen Carl, she would have. Halfway into the car, she pleaded to her husband, 'Perhaps we could stay a few more days?'

'No, I'm sorry, Honey. Get in. I've told you already; we must get this flight. It's the only one with availability this week.'

Mabel joined them for the farewell, and they waved once more until the car disappeared.

They all needed silence to digest the two days' momentous events and revelations. None more than Felicity, who had alternating waves of remorse and relief.

Bruno hadn't deceived her after all. The boy's face in the photograph that haunted her and skewed her judgement, now named by Eva, had inserted a precious piece into the jigsaw of Bruno's life.

Once more, she jumped to the wrong conclusion and tortured herself unnecessarily. She thought, *'Put it firmly behind you and look forward to the promise of rosy horizons opening ahead for all the families.'*

Bruno's deep voice echoed in her mind, *'You must come over to meet the family.'* Felicity thought, *'How strange that his family would come here first.'* She felt swept along on a pre-determined plan, helpless to resist.

Mabel had already felt the deft touch of destiny at work. She put her arm around her niece's shoulder and squeezed it to release her excitement.

Felicity said, 'I'm still worried they will claim Carl. Eva will no doubt ask for a copy of his birth certificate that shows Bruno as the father. It could escalate out of my control, and I'll lose him.'

Mabel responded, 'Rubbish! They want to watch him grow up with his four cousins and family. They are not short of a bob or two. Eva told me Bruno's house is vacant now. The manager retired and moved to the coast, so they thought of letting it. Take it or leave it; a new chapter has opened for you and Carl, so think seriously about being accepted into that welcoming family.'

Felicity outlined the numbers on the golden dog tag with her finger and wondered what the future would hold if she let it play out.

Chapter 27

Carlo and Eva agreed that news of this magnitude should be face-to-face, especially as they wished to share in their sons' delight.

On the aircraft, Carlo slowly sipped his drink and glanced at Eva. Like him, she stared into space. He squeezed her hand, and she turned and gave him a look of deep joy and happiness. Carlo remembered that look of serenity that followed the birth of a child. Eva was reliving the feeling of elation. Let her enjoy this moment, he told himself, before real-life activities take over.

They had hoped that any contact with Bruno would bridge this terrible void in their lives. Carlo couldn't help wondering, *'What if we hadn't come to England? Eva firmly believes in fate; it's certainly beyond coincidence. She's right again!'*

Eva reclined in the aeroplane seat and thought whimsically that one puff from fate had blown away their sorrow. She felt doubly close to this fatherless child. He must be part of their family; there was a shiny new future for him and Felicity in California, and all her relatives were welcome.

Carlo looked over at Eva. Her eyes were closed, but she was still smiling.

Eva's mind was racing, marshalling why Felicity and Carlo junior should come to live with them in America. *'Carl is so like Bruno; their baby photos could easily be confused in years to come.Bruno's house and shares in the business could go to Felicity in trust for their child.'* Her mind raced on; *'Felicity would be an asset in the reception and the new retail tasting area adjoining the vinery, with her graceful looks and charming English accent.'*

Carlo lay back and closed his eyes; the insistent throbbing of the aircraft engine was a fitting accompaniment to the clamour of his thoughts. He was reluctant to sleep, not wanting to dilute the euphoria of being lifted out of despair. *'Now there is another familial stake in the future, a new grandson who looks like Bruno, named Carlo, the only one bearing my name.'* He pondered, *'How wide can Fate's hand reach? Destiny intertwines so many lives.'*

His memory produced a vision of Bruno during the special dinner celebrating the end of Bruno's officer training course. I was sure he would do heroic things, not just get blown up by some stray bomb. How incredible that his dog tag survived. When we saw the vast bomb site for ourselves, it was providence that a small piece of steel would come to light. It laid our minds, if not his body, to rest.

There'll be another set of rules for our new family members. Carl is the centre of their lives, and I hope our involvement with them will go happily. Becoming a grandparent can bring closeness without responsibility. Eva is wise, and she will set the pace.

She fell asleep on the plane, still holding hands with her resting husband, happy they could plan for their future.

Tony and Franco waited at the airport and quietly relaxed with a coffee. Tony said, 'Ma was so excited when she rang with their departure time. I wonder what's happened?'

'Nothing, she's just pleased to be coming home.'

They took their positions near the arrivals area and stared in amazement at the two people who emerged with heads held high, brilliant smiles, and shining eyes. Were these the same two pale people, heads bent, who had left, their hearts heavy with misery?

Carlo asked, 'Is there a quiet area where we can sit before making the journey home?'

The boys glanced quizzically, *'What's going on?'*

Franco said, 'We can find somewhere upstairs to have coffee in the viewing area. Would that do?'

'That sounds great.'

The two boys picked up the luggage and installed the family on a sunny table overlooking the runway.

Tony brought the coffees, 'So what's all the cloak and dagger, quiet corner stuff, then?'

'We have some unexpected news from our travels.' Eva said, beaming at them. It was time to surprise her sons.

Carlo started, 'First, the detectives took us to where they found Bruno's dog tag. A multi-storey building already had foundations laid on the bomb site. Now we've been to the exact place; we're relieved that we could not associate that industrial site with Bruno.'

Eva said, 'We didn't look back, just explored the area and did some sightseeing. Visiting the Cavallo's was uplifting. We slotted together as though it was only last week we saw them. When they commiserated over the loss of Bruno, Lena said, "How has Felicity taken it?" There were blank faces from us.'

Carlo shook his head, 'We knew nothing of her. The detective's only lead was a club where Bruno spent some time. He gave us the owner's details, Mabel Evans, who'd become a close friend of Bruno's. She's since retired and moved to the countryside.'

The boys looked at each other and shrugged, wondering where this story led.

Eva spoke rapidly, 'Her niece was this Felicity that Bruno had been dating. The Cavallo's said they seemed besotted with each other, and he secretly planned to buy an engagement ring on his next leave.'

'Really? So, did you find this mystery girl?' Franco asked.

'Yes! We went to Mabel's house, and she walked in. But you won't believe what happened next.' Eva looked at Carlo and beamed.

'It was so moving to meet Felicity and share her grief. She went into the next room and brought back a child. She has a little boy, Bruno's little boy.' This was too much for Eva, and she started sobbing. 'He's so precious and looks just like him.'

Carlo said, 'It floored us when she said to him, "Meet your grandparents, Carl." It was staggering to see a child, eighteen months old, that looked like our baby, Bruno.'

Franco said, 'So now what - we all play happy families?' He feigned surprise and delight but ground his teeth as he could foresee Bruno's small fortune he'd anticipated being whisked out of his hands.

'No need to be nasty,' said Tony.

Eva said, 'Well, we couldn't just bring him back with us, but Felicity promised to visit and bring him across as soon as possible.'

'Yeah, I bet she will. Eye on the prize.' said Franco.

Carlo scolded, 'No, it's nothing like that. Wait until you meet her.'

They had found the link to Bruno they had hoped to find. But what a connection!

Carlo said, 'To go to England looking for a shrine and find a grandchild is the most exciting thing. We wouldn't have discovered Carl if we hadn't gone. We haven't stopped smiling since. But listen to this, he's called Carlo after me, but they call him Carl!'

Franco looked at his watch pointedly. He'd heard enough. 'Shall we go now? It's quite a drive to the valley. You must be tired.'

Tony studied his parents. *They don't look tired. I've never seen them more alive and animated in my life. Franco's nose has been pushed out once again. He's probably eager to get home and spread the gossip of the new family member.'*

On the journey home, the Ponti's excitedly spoke more about their visit. Tony sat in the back with his mother. He listened to the incidents that pulled them out of the abyss of significant loss while Franco sat silently grinding his teeth and drove. He couldn't wait to tell his wife, Susan, about the latest saga.

He dropped them off and drove home along the dust track like a maniac. He leapt out of the car in the front drive, bounded up the steps, and burst into the kitchen so suddenly that he made Susan jump.

Her natural warm brown wavy hair, cut in a bob, swayed as she spun around to greet him.

'Where's the fire?' she asked.

He grabbed a bar stool and faced her. 'While Ma and Pa were away, everything about the bomb site paled to insignificance when they traced Bruno's girlfriend, and listen to this, Bruno's baby!'

Susan widened her eyes, 'Really? Carry on.' She secretly slipped out of her court shoes. He hated her wearing high heels; being five feet ten, she towered over him. Whenever they fought, or he was being unreasonable, it was a sure way of annoying him, so she stored a couple of pairs at the back of the closet.

'The boy's a spit of Bruno from the photos they showed me. Ma's besotted with him; he's Bruno's replacement now. So carried away, she's already talking about transferring Bruno's house and holdings to this Felicity in trust for her brat.'

Susan choked at that, 'They what? Already talking about wills and stuff?'

Franco agreed, 'The woman had the cheek to call the baby Carlo, shortened to Carl. We'll have to rein in Ma and Pa until we establish the legalities; otherwise, we'll wake up to find our assets transferred to England and a stranger with a leading voice on our board.'

Susan leaned over and poured two glasses of red wine, 'Ain't there something now like a blood test to verify its family?'

'I don't know about that. We'll have to ask around.'

'What does Tony think?'

The words tumbled out of his mouth; he hardly stopped for breath as he sipped the wine. 'He's just as stupid as they are. Anyhow, they'll be visitin' soon, so we can judge for ourselves. Ma and Pa will stump up the fares. All that to-ing and fro-ing will be a bit of a dent in the family finances. Free holidays for the mother and baby, but we'll have to ensure they won't be comin' back.'

Susan chimed in, 'They'll simmer down and accept it's just another grandchild. It's no doubt cheered them and a focus away from Bruno's death.'

Franco didn't look pacified and continued to look on the downside, 'I hope all this doesn't make us cancel our Italian trip. The boys are so damn excited about taking long-haul flights. Their first holiday out of the States.'

They were a strong-willed couple who disappointed both parents with a small registrar's wedding. The Ponti tribe found Susan clever but austere, not given to grand shows of affection.

Franco assisted Carlo in running the firm and seemed to be the natural successor when his father retired. Bruno was more into viniculture research, and Tony seemed settled in his role of accountant and sales. When the States joined in the war with the Allies, Bruno was the natural one to join up because of his medical background and no wife or children to leave behind.

Susan thought, *'He's so fired up and edgy. I hope all this fuss about the child doesn't drag on; I'm bored with it already. These*

Italians are so volatile; I'm glad I kept my distance and avoided being devoured by them.'

To distract him and pull the conversation up, she said, 'We'll educate our boys away from here to give them perspective on the real world, perhaps vacations with European culture.'

Franco droned on, 'To them, Bruno was the tallest, the good-looking and clever son who brought innovations introducing other strains of grape cultures. What always got me was that people peered over and around me to speak to him.'

Susan had heard all this before and humoured him, 'Honey, it's normal for the second child to struggle and try to measure up. Sometimes number one is bossy because they're asked to look after the younger ones and sometimes stand in for the parents.'

She clasped her hands over his to divert him from going down the depression slope, 'Franco, do you remember how we met at University? You took economics, and I did French and English to prepare me for marrying a diplomat or senator.'

'I sure do. Why?'

'When my parents enquired about your family background, I said, 'They're growers.'

Franco laughed as she continued, 'My mother was so shocked, "You mean farmers?" and I replied, "Not really, they are Italian winemakers; they grow grapes. I watched their faces, etched with disbelief, and added, 'In Napa Valley, California." They dreamed of me marrying into boring politics. I'd finally asserted my independence and got them off my back in one fell swoop.'

Franco never tired of the story or her triumphant face and chin lifted in victory.

Susan said, 'We chose freedom, and you could have prospered anywhere with your qualifications, but you wanted to be part of this ambitious dynasty. So, stop comparing yourself with Bruno; you are different types. But just think, you are here and living, whereas he, poor soul, is dead and gone.'

She stood up, pushed him so playfully he nearly toppled off the stool, kissed him tenderly on the lips, undid his top shirt button and slowly replenished their wine. 'I'm off to bed,' She grabbed her glass, turned suggestively towards the door, and started to unzip her cotton slip dress.

Chapter 28

Mabel sat at the kitchen table with Felicity, 'Eva insists we all go over to meet her family. Betsy and I are already planning our packing for a holiday there.'

'What? Packing already? Bruno told me each brother had a pleasant house on the estate, so we'll be comfortable _when_we decide to go.'

'I told Anna about the Ponti's visit. They have holiday entitlements and will come to take care of Amber and the house.'

'That's great, but I'm not sure about going just yet. I'm still worried about the Ponti's taking over Carl.'

'Don't worry. If anyone's taking over, it will be us. Betsy and I are unstoppable. Talk about G.I. brides. They'll wonder what's hit them!'

Felicity went into gales of laughter and said, 'Alright, let's go for a visit. You wicked women, planning behind my back.' Mabel's whirlwind of hope had blown away her worries and replaced them with an air of anticipation for the next phase of their lives. _'What was Bruno's life like over there, and will I fit in?'_

On arrival in California, the heat that welcomed the travellers as they stepped off the plane overwhelmed them. From a chilly autumnal climate, they had stepped into summer once again. Felicity knew right away she'd packed the wrong clothes; she needed a sunhat and sunglasses as a priority.

Betsy was in awe of the enormous cars that filled the airport car park. Carlo's sedan, a four-door Cadillac Series 65, had plenty of room for three adults and the toddler who lay across Felicity's knees. It took a bit of getting used to being driven on the "wrong side" of the road. Once they left the tarmac of the city streets and entered the undulating hillside country, the valley roads became longer and dustier.

Everyone enjoyed spotting the unique buildings, from new stone houses with pitched tiled roofs to simple clapboard, flat-roofed chalets. Carlo said they didn't have snow but occasionally had heavy rains, which contributed to flooding.

As they turned into the dust track leading to the estate, they saw the sizeable handwritten sign, painted in white on dark wood, "Ponti Winery'. They looked at each other, impressed; they couldn't believe they would be here for a fortnight.

'You'll be staying in Bruno's house. It has three bedrooms and is only a short walk from the main house where we congregate most evenings.'

Eva bustled out to greet them, thrilled to welcome the little English family to their home. She was a gracious hostess; she took them walking and sightseeing in the town or along the river every afternoon, pointing out a few well-known wineries on the way. One balmy evening, a few days into their stay, Eva sat with Felicity, facing the sunset in the neat grassy area next to Bruno's house.

Felicity said, 'It's so peaceful here. I love seeing the vineyards stretching out towards the mountains. And the sunsets here are so wide. There's nothing to stop the panorama. It just goes on for miles.'

Eva was pleased to hear Felicity's appreciation of the countryside and decided it was time to ask her a very sensitive question. 'We love having you all here. It thrilled Carlo to have another grandson, and he wants to safeguard him as much as possible.'

Felicity sensed this was going to be a conversation where things might get sticky. 'That's very kind, but we're doing just fine in the UK.'

'Yes, I saw how comfortable you are living with Mabel.' She hoped Felicity might spill some more about her set-up.

'My Aunt has been a tower of strength to me all my life. It was only natural that we move in with her when the club closed and she bought Thistledown.'

'You must depend on her quite a lot financially, as you don't seem to have your own house or a job.'

Felicity bristled with indignation; she was out of her depth, just a country girl at heart now floundering in a monied family in

America. To cover up her insecurity, she said, 'Money has never been a driving force for me.'

Eva held up her hands in submission. 'Oh, I'm sorry. I didn't mean to pry.'

'Yes, you did.' Felicity shot back.

The situation got a little heated, but both parties toned down, knowing they had to get along for Carl's sake.

Eva had challenged Felicity's unknown, powerful side and immediately backed down. *'She's no walkover. I admire that.'* She approached the subject head-on and leant forward to seem sincere, 'Carlo just wants to ensure that you and Carl are well provided for, that's all.'

Felicity nodded, 'I'm okay, and if you really need to know, I have enough savings from the sale of the club, and we live with Aunt Mabel because she has no other family members, and I'm to inherit the farm when she dies.'

Eva was taken aback at the sudden transparency and chanced it by adding, 'So you wouldn't mind if Carl is added into Carlo's will?'

She sighed at Eva's tenacity and gave in. 'Eva, who am I to prevent Carl from his inheritance and the kindness of this family?'

Eva sat back in her chair. Mission accomplished. As the sun's rays kissed the mountain tops goodnight, she wondered, *'When can I bring up the subject of his schooling over here?'*

Felicity's feathers had been ruffled, *'They mean well and may wish to include Carl in the family estate, but there's no way he's being educated over here.'*

One lunchtime, Betsy wandered into the vineyard office and watched Tony filing away the paperwork. 'Hello, you look busy.'

Tony looked up, 'Thankfully. We're on a roll now, but it's taken a generation with a ton of problems to get where we are.'

'What sort of problems?'

'My grandparents planted the first vines here, and over a hundred wineries followed not long after. That brought stiff competition and, of course, a surplus of grapes. Tragically, eighty per cent of the valley's vineyards succumbed to phylloxera, the most destructive insect pest that affected the roots.'

It enthralled Betsy to hear the vineyard's chequered history. 'Carry on.'

'It took years, but the family pulled together and recovered to make a decent living for a while. It was tough work replanting and grafting onto the unaffected vines. But I remember that in 1920, Prohibition came in and stopped wine production for about thirteen years. Ma and Pa were really worried, but they bought more land cheaply from those whose businesses didn't survive. On this new land, we tore out any failing grapes and replaced them with apple, fig and walnut orchards.'

'That was a brave thing to do. Trying something new.'

'It was hard work, but we had no choice. The other valley vineyards had an income supplying the local churches with their sacramental wine. They turned to produce some non-alcoholic wine, grape juice or vinegar which was still lawful.'

'But your vineyard now looks so successful. What was the turning point?'

'That diversification. We could sell more than just wine. Throughout those trying times, Pa often discussed the difficulties of wine production with other vineyard owners. So last year, the few surviving vineyards agreed that working together would be more profitable, and they signed an agreement of association. That was the best thing to have happened, and our future looks extremely promising.'

'It must be great to work here with many aspects of the business. For me, it would be one hell of a change from sitting behind a machine in a crowded, noisy factory.'

'Perhaps you'd like to help me set up the tasting rooms and check the wine stocks while you're here?'

Betsy jumped at it. 'I'd love to. When can I start?'

'Let me show you around.' They spent the afternoon preparing for the late afternoon visitors.

As they passed the laboratory at the back of the tasting room, Tony looked wistful, 'Bruno was the one who was interested in new wine production, unique blends and vintages. He was never happier when ensconced with mixing and designing new labels.'

'You must miss him terribly. He talked fondly about this vineyard and his family, but we never really thought we'd visit. My mum was so smitten with him. We can't believe what happened.'

Tony poured a glass of wine for them and raised his glass, 'Here's to new beginnings.'

Chapter 29

Gina instantly took to Felicity and could see what Bruno found so attractive. Felicity confided that she had brought inappropriate winter clothing, not knowing how warm California would be in September. Gina wanted to make her feel wanted and took her to the few local shops to find suitable light clothes and sandals for her stay. 'I'm sorry there's nothing here that suits you, but perhaps we could take a day trip to San Francisco. There's bound to be a better selection. Since the war ended, people have been dressing up more in the city. Last month, there was a huge celebration on Market Street. I didn't go, but the photographs were in the newspaper.'

When Carlo heard from Tony that Gina and Felicity were going shopping in the city, he opened the safe in the office and pulled out a brown envelope full of dollar bills. 'Give this to Gina and ensure Felicity has a lovely time. She's not to pay for anything while she's here.'

Tony counted the notes, slipped them into his back pocket, and laughed. 'They'll think it's Thanksgiving come early.'

While Eva set the table, Felicity helped prepare the vegetables for the family dinner. They had grown much closer over the week, and Carl had enjoyed so much attention from everyone.

Eva said, 'Do you have to go back next week with Mabel and Betsy? I'd love you to stay a little longer to meet Franco, Susan and their boys, but they don't return from their holiday for another few weeks.'

Felicity was getting used to Californian weather, and she didn't have anything to rush home to England for. Betsy would return to the garment factory, and Mabel wanted to return to Amber and her growing social life in Marple. She had enjoyed Gina's company and the novelty of being treated to things, regardless of cost. With her frugal upbringing, she felt wicked but enjoyed their extravagance. Perhaps another few weeks here being pampered wouldn't be so bad after all.

During her last week, Betsy immersed herself in learning the various wines and loved meeting the wholesalers who came to try the latest from the vineyard.

One taster was also a friend of Tony's. He sat opposite Betsy and tried a new red wine. 'This is very good. I can certainly recommend this one to my customers.'

'What do you do?'

I'm Pedro, a wholesaler, and I travel between Sacramento and the San Francisco Bay Area here. I take them some bottles to try, and the customers order through me.

'That's a lot of area to cover. Do you have many vineyards to visit?

'Yes, it's all picking up really well now the war has finished. Hotels and restaurants are getting back to normal.'

Betsy looked at this good-looking twenty-something. He was smartly dressed, sporting the fashionable crew cut associated with power and success. She wanted to know more about him, 'How did you get into all this?'

'My parents, like Tony's, worked hard and long and urged me to take my education seriously because many rewarding jobs are allied to the wineries. I like wine, cars and driving around this countryside meeting clients, so it's the perfect job for me.'

'It certainly seems like it. I work in a clothes factory in the North of England. Nothing could be further than this way of life.'

'I didn't catch your name?'

'Betsy'

'That's pretty.'

'Mum named me in memory of my delicate grandmother that I never met.'

He quickly changed the subject. 'Do you like wine?'

'I wasn't keen until I came here, but Tony's been teaching me the merits. The funny thing is that I can drink alcohol in the UK at eighteen, but you must be twenty-one here. So, I won't be legal in the USA until next May.'

'I can sense you'll have a big party here for that one.'

'I'm afraid I'll be back in the UK by the end of next week. But don't worry, I'll still have a party for my 21st, wherever I may be.

When Tony's brother, Bruno, told us he was a grape grower, we imagined bunches of grapes grown high on walls and glasshouses. We didn't expect whole hillsides of them.'

'Some people still cultivate them like that, but mainly as shade on the sides of glass houses. It's excellent vineyard land, loam slopes and gravel soil. Zinfandel is popular here, and a steamship used to travel frequently between San Francisco and Napa. They called it the Zinfandel Steamer!'

'You're kidding.'

'It's all true. There's a lot of history here.'

Pedro looked over at Tony, who raised his eyebrows. Pedro smiled and deliberately turned his attention to Betsy. There seemed to be some easy connection between them. Pedro decided to change meetings and hang around Napa for a few more days before heading for the Bay area.

After the tasting, Betsy asked Tony about Pedro. 'Is he a good sort? Not always after the ladies?'

'Oh, he's harmless. I've known him since school. He's committed to getting the best wines for his customers, and no one has a bad word to say about him. He's kind, generous and charming but dresses a bit too formal for around here, but he likes to make a good impression wherever he goes. As he says, he never knows who his next customer might be.'

'He's a salesman who's never off duty, then?'

'You could say that. However, his hobby is cars. He's always tinkering about, fixing up some snazzy auto he's found and turning a profit.'

'So, he goes from one extreme to the other; natty dresser to oil-stained overalls. He's very nice. I like talking to him.'

'I think he's quite smitten with you too.'

Chapter 30

When Susan and Franco returned from Italy, they were disconcerted to find Felicity and Carl happily installed in Bruno's house.

Franco confided in Susan, 'In Pa's will, Bruno's part of this estate will now be divided between Tony and me. This will give our boys a huge nest egg and set them up for life. We must ensure this Felicity doesn't stay here long with the boy. We must be careful though, mustn't question anything, as Ma and Pa seem besotted with their new grandchild, their replacement Bruno.'

Susan said, 'I'm sure you'll protect our interests, but let's wait a while and see what happens.'

Franco was impatient. 'I don't want an interloper taking my hard-earned cash and rightful inheritance. The boy might look like him, but without proof, they could be tricksters trying it on. I might have them investigated.'

Without delay, Franco consulted a lawyer, who confirmed what Susan said. 'Don't upset your parents yet. You can afford to wait.'

There was still a niggling doubt that Felicity was a gold digger with an eye on a wealthy American. These thoughts messed with his mind, and he cursed fate for disrupting the balance of power between his brothers.

The week flew by, and at the airport, Betsy clung tearfully to her mother, who said, 'You are silly; we'll see you in a few weeks.'

'I know, but it's all been so perfect. I really like it here in the States.'

Mabel offered her an embroidered handkerchief to blow her nose. To change the subject, she said, 'Anna and Frank will meet us at the airport. Have you got your photos safe to show them?'

Gina edged her way to the rim of the little gang; her eyes scanned the crowd. Slightly away from the group, a man she didn't recognise leaned against the wall. She quickly assessed him as of

Mediterranean origin, smartly dressed in his mid-twenties. He was staring intently at Betsy.

Betsy looked back towards the family for the last wave and spotted him. Her mouth opened with amazement, and she gave a broad smile and frantic wave of recognition. His serious face lit up, and he blew her a kiss.

Gina glanced at Betsy, who was now blushing as she waved to her mother again. Gina looked down as Eddy was standing next to her, clutching his balloon, and when she looked back, the stranger had gone. 'Who was he? Betsy certainly seemed to know him!'

Mabel was relieved to sit back in her seat on the plane. As she dozed, she promised herself a long rest, pottering in the garden until the dust settled. After they took off and the flight levelled out, the hostess asked, 'Would you like a drink, Madam?'

Mabel looked at Betsy and confidently ordered, 'Zinfandel for two, please.' There'd be no half-lager for her anymore. She was becoming sophisticated in her old age.

Betsy giggled and nudged her great-aunt, who said, 'All this emotion is killing me.'

Carlo had insisted on buying them upgraded tickets with the instructions, 'You'll need some sleep. It's a very long journey.'

Betsy sipped her wine, 'I can get used to this lifestyle.'

'It's all been like an amazing dream. Wake me up when I get to Marple.'

Chapter 31

Anna sat opposite Betsy, Mabel and Frank, watching and listening. So much was unfolding about their mother, Carl, and the American family. It had been such a whirlwind for them that it would be a relief to get back to normality while they digested what had happened. Amber, the spaniel, was glad to get all his guardians back and return to a routine.

Betsy didn't slot back easily into her English life after her holiday. She felt dissatisfied and lost. *'How can a few days unsettle me like this? I'd gone out with Mum and Carl as support, but I love the Californian lifestyle and the weather.'*

She perked up the following week when she received a postcard from Pedro depicting the iconic Golden Gate Bridge. He'd written the words 'Ciao Bella', which the Italians wrote affectionately on all their cards.

Mabel and Anna were intrigued when they saw the card. Betsy explained, 'He was a customer. I only met him a few times in the winery shop with Tony, who must have given Pedro my address.' She deliberately omitted the bit about seeing him at the airport send-off.

At home, the family shared and picked over every minor incident in America. But at work, it was a complex and different scenario. Betsy thought, *'Here I am, stuck in a boring, stuffy building for hours. I can't even talk about America to the others because it looks like I'm showing off. I have to downplay everything. It's a long shot, but I need to look for any job opportunity to get back there.'*

Eva and Tony discussed how well Mabel and Betsy's visit had gone and, particularly, Betsy's enthusiasm for running the winery. Tony said, 'She would certainly be an asset to us, and we'd be keeping it all in the family.'

'If she came back to work here, that would be another pull for Felicity and Carl to stay or visit more often.'

'So, we need an excuse to get her here before she gets snapped up in England. I think my ankle already hurts.'

She joked, 'It does look a bit swollen; do you think you might have wrenched it? You might be walking with a limp out of here.'

'It gets more painful just thinking about it!'

'Perhaps you could do with resting it and need some help in the office? You probably need someone to do the running around in the tasting room. A suitable person wouldn't have to know so much about the wine, but if they are a quick study, all the better.'

'Know anyone who might fit the bill and would be able to drop everything at a moment's notice? I can tell you a few customers have been asking after Betsy because they thought she was a permanent fixture.'

'Perhaps we could ask Felicity; she might know someone.' They cackled at their scheme to get Betsy back.

Felicity was hanging out some washing when Eva approached her, and in tow was Tony, with a pronounced limp and his face contorted in pain.

'Oh Tony, what have you done?

'I've wrenched my ankle pulling some cases of wine out of the store. I was stupid, it was too heavy, and I stumbled.'

Eva casually said, 'He'll be laid up for a while and can only be seated doing the accounts. We're in a pickle without someone trusted to run the tasting room. Carlo might take over, but he finds customer-facing jobs rather wearing.'

Tony perked up, 'I have an idea. Felicity, do you think Betsy would come back and help me out? She was very interested in that side of things.'

Felicity looked at both of them and instantly knew what they were up to. 'Put an ice pack on that ankle and rest for a while.'

Eva looked worried as if their plan could backfire, but Felicity added, 'I'm sure she could be spared from the factory as it's such an emergency.' She shook her head in disbelief at their machinations.   Tony and Eva knew they had been rumbled and looked at each other, and Tony shrugged.

'Who's going to call her and give her such distressing news?' Felicity said, smiling as she latched onto the scheme.

Eva piped up, 'I can do it. I want a word with Mabel anyway.'

That evening, Tony limped theatrically into their kitchen and grimaced at Gina.

'Oh no. Go and sit down in the other room.' Gina said, helping him into the sitting room.

'Thanks. It's a nasty sprain that's just come on.' With a broad grin, he flopped onto the sofa, 'I've got to take it easy until Betsy gets here.'

'Betsy? What's she got to do with anything?'

'It just so happens that she'll be free to come back and help me out. Such a useful girl. Pedro will be able to keep her amused in the evenings so that she won't be too bored.'

Gina looked amazed. 'What on earth is going on?'

'Eva wanted another hold over Felicity, so we've concocted this sham. It might just work too.'

'You schemers. So, nothing's wrong with your ankle then?'

Tony wiggled his foot, 'Em, just a temporary setback until she's on the flight. Carlo will be able to help her as he's getting bored with his retirement. He won't mind in the slightest.'

'What have you to gain if she comes back?'

'If she returns permanently, that will release me to share the managerial side with Franco. At the moment, Franco is doing it all; knowing him, he'll wheedle himself into the top job and take over the whole winery.'

Gina said, So everybody gains apart from Franco. That's a good plan.'

Tony said, 'Pedro's going to be so pleased as he spent quite some time with Betsy and even showed up at the airport departures.'

'I saw someone blow a kiss to her and couldn't fathom out who on earth it was. Now it's all clear; he's a friend of yours.'

A few days after their return to Marple, Eva telephoned Mabel, who contacted the long-distance operator first as it was the first overseas call she had made. Mabel was thrilled to hear from her. They exchanged pleasantries through the crackle and slight delay, and then Eva asked to speak to Betsy, who listened intently and then screamed, 'Yes! I'd love to,' jumped up and down with delight and passed the phone to Mabel.

'What's all this excitement about?' Mabel asked Eva.

'Tony has wrenched his ankle and is hopping about the winery. Betsy impressed him with her enjoyment and learning about the tasting shop. She didn't sound enamoured with her present job in England, so Tony thought she might like to come back here to help and do his running about. Of course, we'll pay all her expenses, and there's plenty of room for her with Felicity and Carl in Bruno's house. Felicity thought it was perfect and, of course, would love her company. The customers have already been asking about her, which gave Tony the idea. What do you think?'

Mabel said, 'No doubt about it. She's obviously thrilled to be asked. After visiting you, she never really settled down, always talking about California.' She laughed. 'I expect she's already gone to pack. We'll sort out another visa and travel bookings tomorrow and let you know.'

Betsy sat on her bed and inwardly prayed her gratitude, *'Someone up there has been listening. I've missed Mum and little Carl. Weird to think he has more relatives over there than here. I can't wait to get back to all the action going on in Napa.'*

A week later, a bleary-eyed Mabel saw an excited Betsy off at dawn, and many weary hours later, it was Pedro who welcomed her to sunny San Francisco again.

When Pedro told his parents he was going to pick up Tony's relative from the airport arriving from England, they exchanged questioning glances. Only a special lady would warrant a round trip of three hours.

His mother said, 'What's her name? I would love to meet her. I love the English accent. Is it too soon to ask her for dinner tomorrow evening?'

'Thank you, Ma, I'll ask. Her name is Betsy. She's lovely, and I think you'll like her. I met her last month at Tony's.' He strutted to the garage, and began singing merrily as he polished his car again. His parents watched and chuckled at their son's antics, obviously smitten with this English lady.

It surprised Betsy that it was only Pedro meeting her at the airport. He explained after stowing her luggage and helping her into the front seat of the sparkling Ford Coupe convertible. 'Carlo is still helping Tony, who is hopping around, and Felicity thought the trip was too long, both ways in one day, so I offered to pick you up.'

She smiled at him. 'You're a lovely surprise, and I must thank you so much for the postcard. It gave me such a boost and confirmed my visit wasn't all made up.'

'I'm glad you got it. I thought you'd like a reminder of your holiday, but I honestly never expected you back so soon.'

'Neither did I,' she smiled and sat back in the stylish red car, ready for the mid-afternoon drive. Pedro drove carefully and slowly, pointing out places of interest in the countryside. She felt like a film star with her sunglasses on and blonde hair wafting in the warm sun. It wasn't long before they entered the familiar undulating scenery of flourishing grape vines.

'How long d'ya think you're staying this time?'

'I suppose it depends on Tony's ankle.'

'My folks live in the next valley to Carlo. Ma's invited you to dinner tomorrow if you're not too tired from travelling. She wants to see and hear this lovely English lady in person.'

'I'd love to meet her, and I'd better stay up later tonight to avoid the time lag.'

'Ah, here we are.' He honked as they pulled up outside the estate's main house.

He helped her out of the car and placed her luggage on the dusty driveway. 'Have a nice rest, and I'll pick you up at seven tomorrow.' She waved, and as she watched him zoom off, she thought, *'Are all men in California dark, attractive and have amazing cars?'*

Eva and Carlo came rushing out of the large archway. Carlo hugged Betsy warmly and picked up her suitcase. Eva took her arm, and they marched into the refreshingly cool house.

Betsy pulled up a lounge chair and slumped next to Tony, who rested his bandaged foot on a low stool. Eva and Carlo joined them with glasses of chilled fruit juice.

Betsy said, 'I had a lovely drive up. Pedro's so chatty. He's invited me to dinner tomorrow night at his parent's house. He's picking me up at seven. I hope that's okay with you?'

Tony pretended to look incredulous. 'Pedro? He's not chatty with me, and he'd probably look more appealing if he smiled more. Ah, he's not that bad; he has a good brain, but he boasts about being such a stylish dresser. He winked at Eva, and they both knew their plans had worked. Felicity's daughter is here now and probably won't return for a while, if at all.

Carlo looked at his watch. 'We've got an hour. Let's have coffee, and then I'll remind you where everything is at the office and take you to your mother; she'll be waiting.'

Eva walked over to Felicity to let her know Betsy had arrived safely. 'Carlo will bring her over shortly. She's only been here five minutes and already booked up. Having dinner tomorrow with Pedro's parents in the next valley.'

Felicity said, 'Do you think something's going on there? He was quick to offer to pick her up at the airport. Crafty devil. He's trying to beat any opposition before they knew the game had begun.'

Eva smiled, *Felicity doesn't miss a trick. But this is only one trick in a whole card game.*

When Tony brought Betsy to the house, he said to Felicity, Pedro's also a great car mechanic, with nice shirts and pants. Poor sweet Betsy doesn't stand a chance, especially if he finds her a sports car,' and they laughed at the prospect.

Chapter 32

Eighteen months earlier in Manchester, although the Blitz had been over for some time, the new menace to South-East Britain was doodlebugs. These were radio-controlled flying bombs. The enemy had two attempts to reach Manchester; one landed on the outskirts of a small town, and the second one just missed its target, the Royal Exchange railway station, and hit the nearby building.

The bomb fell without warning. Fine brick dust was strewn everywhere. The trained men knew their priority was speed to find survivors on the bomb sites. They started to stretcher away a few dead bodies for identification. Their job was more accessible by the powdery rubble and fine weather. In the early evening, the workers hurried home to avoid the blackout. Some stopped to stare at the bright lights in the darkness brought by recovery teams to work through the night. The bomb disposal unit and personnel worked slowly, hoping for a miracle, to find people alive when they heard, 'Here! Over here!'

Their spirits lifted when they gently prised two more men out of the dust piles. When the shout 'They're alive!' echoed around the site, they all rushed and gathered, ready to help if required. A shot of adrenaline surged through the workers' aching bodies. The paramedic shouted, 'They've had a lucky escape, one broken arm, a bump on the head, and the other beggar will just have bruises.'

The recovery leader called out to his team, 'Thank you, lads. Two men will return to their families tonight because of your efforts. That's it. Get this bally light out.'

He looked around at the faces greyed with fatigue from late afternoon work into the evening. Some had lines where tears of emotion had slipped down their dusty cheeks. He said, 'There'll be another crew here at dawn. Go home, lads, and wash that dust away. Well done. Goodnight.'

The medics at the hospital took the two men into cubicles. One patient was easily identified from the wallet inside his jacket. He was a commuter waiting for a train. Miraculously, he only sustained bruises from falling masonry, and after a check-up and some time allowed for shock, they discharged him.

One man moaned as he lapsed into and out of consciousness. An initial assessment showed he had suffered a massive blow to the head, and blood still trickled down his face onto his neck from the nasty gash. They also discovered a broken right arm and splinted it. Someone looked in his torn leather wallet for identification, but it only held the remnants of two fifty-pound notes. The tattered leisurewear clung to his body, and the ripped pockets yielded no further clue to his identity. His old gold wristwatch smashed in the explosion hung around his wrist by the clasp.

After a few days, he had not gained full awareness, and they transferred him to a long-stay psychiatric unit in Macclesfield. It was a large old manor house with giant oak trees dotted around the grounds. Extra wings built over time and necessity didn't spoil the impressive facade. There were no medical or operating facilities; it was purely psychiatric treatment and convalescence.

Dr Ian Kirk surveyed his new patient. On a clipboard, he made copious notes; olive skin, thick black hair, and judging by his soft hands, long supple fingers with manicured nails, he was not a manual worker. He inspected the stitches holding together the large cut on his patient's forehead.

He said to the nurse, 'I guess he's about forty. Well-toned body from gym or sport. We'll know more when he comes round and starts talking.'

The nurse looked down at the black eyelashes, arched eyebrows, and regular features. She raised her eyebrows with a wry smile and a wicked voice. 'He's handsome. I can't wait for him to surface!'

Bruno lay still for a few days, then opened his sticky eyes and blinked, forcing them to focus. The smell of disinfectant was overpowering, so he closed them. He heard a man's voice, 'Don't worry, mate. You're in a hospital; we're taking care of you.'

He kept his eyes closed, and his left hand crossed his right arm. It felt restricted with the splint. His hand reached over his forehead, where he fingered the padding, which started above his left eye and ran into his hairline. The man's voice said, 'A nasty gash there, and you'll need some physio on that broken arm.'

A little while later, he pulled open his eyes and was inches away from a cheerful smiling face of a female nurse peering down at him, waving a plastic beaker of water. 'Hello, glad you're back with us. Small sips to start.'

The cool drink poured into his dry mouth as he sucked the straw.

'Blown up and pulled out of the rubble, you were. What's your name, Sir.' she said in a soft, heavily accented Mancunian voice.

There was no answer. An older man butted in, 'Must be the head wound.' They nodded in concurrence as the patient slipped off into oblivion.

The nurses talked to him continuously in case something jogged him to talk. 'They sent you here from Manchester. You're in a long-stay military hospital in Macclesfield. We're waiting for your memory and speech to return as you recover from the trauma. We've called you John Doe for now.'

They were just words to Bruno, with no meaning. Over a few weeks, he slowly regained strength; and they removed the plaster on his arm, ready for physio. A light dressing covered the stitches on his forehead.

At his first look in the mirror, he lifted the dressing, but it wasn't the scar that horrified him; it was his beautifully groomed hair. The orderlies had played hairdresser, scissored their way around his scalp and shaped it into a thatch of badly cut, ragged edges. He resembled a poorly cut, curly black terrier.

Bruno required help with his daily shower and wet shave, being right-handed. He had tried using his left hand, but the nurses felt it too dangerous to let him continue after a few bloody nicks.

He still hadn't spoken a word, but the nurses continued to banter as his eyes followed their lips, trying to make sense of what they were saying.

His arm soon mended, and a nurse removed his forehead stitches, leaving an angry scar across his temple. His mind searched for comfort and automatically remembered actions beyond washing and dressing.

Dr Kirk, the psychiatrist, was particularly interested in him. Although Bruno was still mute and a walking wounded, he slowly helped around the hospital. It seemed natural to him to be assisting in this environment. The clinical ambience and disinfectant smell were familiar. He made himself helpful in tending to patients by delivering and collecting food trays and ensuring fresh water was available.

More experience in the medical sphere slowly surfaced. When the hospital became overwhelmed with patients, Bruno was willing to work any hours on the severely shell-shocked men. Field hospitals sent long-term patients from North Africa, Burma, and the front line in Northern France. Without speaking, he helped bathe and feed them and gently turn them to avoid bed sores if they were bed-bound.

The staff trusted him and were pleased to have more willing hands. He had already moved into the staff accommodation and worked almost full-time, and someone suggested he should have some wages. They enlisted him in the ranks of the paid orderlies until his memory and voice returned.

One evening, an orderly was brought up with a start as Bruno started to sing along to the radio. It was a Neapolitan folk song, and he sang it in faultless Italian. It was exciting; this was their first clue to his identity. He alerted Dr Kirk, who dropped everything and hurried to hear this. Their John Doe was unaware they were trying to place his nationality and continued singing along with the radio. He was thrilled with this sudden breakthrough in his memory.

Dr Kirk phoned the Italian Embassy. 'I'm calling from the psychiatric hospital in Macclesfield. A patient wounded in an air raid has regained some memory, and we've heard him singing along to Italian folk songs. This may be a clue to his identity; perhaps you'd like to investigate further if I give you a description?'

The Embassy had nothing and contacted the Home Office, who eagerly searched their records. An Italian agent might be valuable fodder for exchanging foreign spies.

What Bruno thought was special care and compassion became covert surveillance. The authorities drafted a bogus Neapolitan patient to befriend him, but he had no luck finding out more.

160

He certainly didn't have their natural mannerisms and wild hand gestures, so they concluded he was not pure Italian. Their John Doe still had amnesia and didn't talk, but the long-term prognosis was fair.

The other orderlies looked after him and taught him all the hospital routines. They were his lifeline. He was still their own charge; they were responsible for him as a long-term patient. Being much older than them, they soon treated him with unconscious deference, with an innate feeling of his superior education and refinement.

The psychiatric nurses had learned to accept the long passage of recovery time for some patients. The weeks turned into months as their John Doe made good physical progress.

Bruno joined the other orderlies at the local cinema. Working with them, he managed to speak a few sentences of English, which came with a smooth American accent. The nurses hoped the patient might be a film star, but the authorities thought differently. Their more realistic concept was that he might be a mole living in the States and sent here to spy, but he got caught up in the bombing. They discounted nothing in wartime and took no chances. Firstly, Italian folksongs, now American, with an accent, probably picked up at the movies; which role would he assume next, Russian?

Dr Kirk continued to spend time with this working patient. His choice of English words, medical knowledge and good manners pointed to a middle-class background. He dismissed the spy theory and became more attached to John Doe. His progress was slow but had improved dramatically from the total blank on arrival.

Bruno's immediate colleagues were briefed. 'Keep him from overworking; he is very dedicated. Continue your psychiatric training, take him on your little outings', and he pointed outside, 'Sit amongst our lovely grounds. Sometimes it only takes one thing to stimulate the memory. Show him pictures of well-known buildings in the USA. Something might come forward.'

On a sunny Saturday, Bruno enjoyed a day out at Belle Vue Zoo and the amusement park with a couple of paramedics. He was adamant he would have a ride on the big dipper. This was the first time they had seen him so animated and determined. The lads debated letting him go on the winding, towering contraption.

'It can't do any harm,' they joked. 'It might shake him up and bring back some of his memory.'

On the downward speed of the open carriage, Bruno laughed and shrieked with the other children. He wondered why he enjoyed this so much and felt such emotional strength. Something exciting was attached to the park, but he had no idea what; nothing seemed to make sense at the moment.

The men had time to wander around the zoo before dusk and made their way to the exit. They stopped to peer through the wire mesh of the elephant enclosure.

A few people queued, waiting to board the seat contraption strapped to its back as it kneeled. Bruno could sense the novelty for the people laughing and shuffling along. The elephant's twinkly eyes transfixed on him, peeping out from the sea of grey crinkled skin, and it raised its trunk in recognition.

One lad looked at Bruno, 'You've got a friend here. We'll go on that next time.'
Bruno uncurled his fingers reluctantly from the wire and followed the others. He glanced over his shoulder and thought, *'There's something about that elephant.'*

Two stops before Piccadilly, they dropped down and doubled back to the chip shop. A scrubbed wooden table and two long benches invited them to eat fish and chips on the premises, but customers usually took away the shop's offerings. They used the edges of the chip-wrapping newspaper to clean their greasy fingers before they screwed them up into balls and had a contest to see who threw and got them directly in the bin. They then dodged the traffic to cross the road. Bruno thought, *'We reach the pavement and turn right, past the gift kiosk and tobacconist, up the approach. All this is so familiar to me. Why?'*

Bruno felt queasy as they walked to the London Road Station for their train to Macclesfield. This stretch of road was familiar, and he stopped and looked into shop windows, playing for time to recover from the shock of recognising the area. As they waited for the train, Bruno walked around the busy station and identified the

162

various features, including the small gift shop and the newsagent. Instinct warned him not to tell the others, but he vowed to return on his own and see if he could trigger more memories.

The first train stop was Macclesfield, so the lads had time for a brief nap. Bruno wasn't tired, but he closed his eyes and tried to remember every little detail of the area near the station. He concentrated on controlling his fast breathing, hyperventilation brought on by excitement from the recognition. He wondered, *'Why was the station approach familiar? Could it be a sign of my recovery?'* Bruno stared at the passing green countryside but felt conflicted, exhilarated by the breakthrough, but could he trust his memory?

Dr Kirk noticed that Bruno had perked up after the outing with the lads; he was smiling more and talkative. A few days later, Paul, an orderly, had reason to go to Manchester, and Bruno asked, 'Can I come too?'

Paul needed new clothes, and while he was in a cubicle trying on trousers, Bruno quickly lost him in the big department store, nipped outside and strode in the direction he previously recognised. The street was undoubtedly familiar, and he kept walking, hoping to come across something else familiar. He stopped dead in his tracks when he came across the club on a side street. His heart pounded as memories cascaded, but something was wrong with the place. He stared at photos of beat groups plastered outside and didn't recognise the interior, which showed a stage. The place he remembered was an area to play pool and a cosy bar, nothing resembling a nightclub.

Bitterly disappointed, he couldn't reconcile these pictures to what he recalled: a simple servicemen's club with mismatched furniture and tall windows.

There was no sign of life around until a workman in brown overalls, carrying a bag of tools, came out and locked the club door. He lit a cigarette and joined Bruno, who was studying the adverts and looking perplexed.

'Hi mate, I helped to set it up,' he said proudly, puffing on his cigarette. 'It's a busy nightclub with small groups of musicians on the weekend. My friend Mabel ran it as a club for years, so I still get called out for minor maintenance. If you want to go in, it opens at eight every night. You'll enjoy it. Local bands, but they're good.'

Bruno pressed his hands together, trying to keep calm as hazy memories emerged from his trapped memory bank. 'Mabel? Is she a taller, older lady, quite a feisty one?'

The worker replied, beaming and enthusiastic. 'Yes, that sounds like her. Are you American? Did you come here when it was a serviceman's club?

'Yeah, I think I did,' Bruno said, wondering if that statement was true.

'She's retired now and lives in the country.'

Excited at discovering another clue, Bruno desperately wanted to find this Mabel. 'Where exactly does she live?'

'Marple. I can give you an address. I bet she'd love to get a card from you from the States.' He fished out a grubby business card and scribbled her address on the back. 'You're a long way from home. Enjoy the rest of your stay. Thanks for your service.' He jumped into his van and slowly accelerated to the main road. He had noted the long scar and knew it was a war injury, and he was undoubtedly skinny for his six-foot frame.

Bruno studied the card, 'Bill Briggs, Builder and Maintenance'; Mabel's name and address were on the back. He glanced at his watch, hurried the five minutes to the station, sat on a bench near the entrance, and waited. Two minutes later, Paul arrived, laden with department store bags.

A relieved Paul said, 'So sorry I lost you in that store. It's massive. I hoped you might make it back here. Dr Kirk would have had something to say if I returned without you. Our train's due in five minutes; the platform's over there,' and he pointed to the right.

Bruno felt wicked as he realised his mind was working much better and said, 'No problem. I slowly made my way back here, looking at the shops. I knew you'd catch me up. It looks like you bought up the store.'

'Yes, I got what I came for and more,' he laughed.

On the train, Bruno touched the card in his jacket pocket. He vaguely remembered Mabel. But who was she, and why remember her? What was I doing at her club?

Bruno's supervision at the hospital had become oppressive for the first time. Since his trips out, he had slowly unravelled a few strands of his identity and wanted to follow the few clues independently. *'I don't want to live anymore as the hospital's paper cut out, with a pseudonym. I have to find Mabel. She'll know who I really am. I've got to get out of here, but alone.'*

Chapter 33

Bruno counted the stash of notes and coins in his wallet. Mentally prepared, he would wait for an opportunity to present itself and didn't have long to wait. The next day, as he helped an outgoing patient into a cab, he asked the driver, 'I have friends in Marple. How far is it from here, and how much would it cost to go there?'

The cabbie replied, 'It's easy from here; to avoid the city, take a taxi straight there; it only costs you two quid, and you could return by train to Manchester and another train here.' Bruno offered him a coin with thanks, but he waved it away. 'You're all doing a grand job in there.'

Bruno smiled and thought, 'Nice folk around here.' He would eventually learn the helpful lesson that cab drivers pride themselves on their local geographical knowledge and, in fact, everything else in life.

On his day off, he said to Paul, 'I'm going down to Macclesfield,' and laughed as he added, 'I could always flag an ambulance back up.'

Paul said, 'Who's going with you? You can't go on your own. You haven't been signed off.'

Bruno hadn't thought it mattered as he was treated as one of the staff and could probably come and go as he pleased. This was not so; he had to be sly and slip out.

A short way out, a taxi passed him on the other side of the road. He was dropping off a visitor at the hospital. Bruno lifted his finger and pointed backwards. A thumbs-up from the driver secured his transport. When it returned, he got in the cab, and they drove away while he searched for the card. 'Marple, please.'

'Okay, mate, off we go.'

Bruno gazed out at the verdant countryside; he felt at home with fields and crops. They travelled as far as the large roundabout and went right round, taking the road back to the hospital lodge. Bruno became worried and agitated, wondering what was going on.

The cabbie turned to Bruno at the entrance and said, 'Hang on just a minute, I've forgotten something.' He leapt out and strode over to the porter's lodge. He stayed there until Dr Kirk joined him.

The cabbie said, under his breath, 'I've found one of your loonies escaping. He was going to Marple with no address.'

Dr Kirk couldn't believe it was Bruno in the back of the cab and signalled for him to get out. It zoomed off, leaving them both at the porter's lodge.

He led Bruno to his office. 'What was all that about? Why Marple, and on your own?'

Bruno was cagey. 'It's just a name I heard that seemed to ring a bell, and I thought I'd go there to see if it triggered anything. That's all.'

'Why didn't you ask someone to go with you?'

'I just wanted to do something on my own and not waste anyone's time.'

Dr Kirk wrote in his notes, '*John Doe:Excellent progress today. The first initiative he has shown since his arrival.*'

Bruno leaned against the office door, not wanting to linger longer than necessary. Dr Kirk suggested, 'You're just in time for lunch if you hurry.'

He played with his cottage pie in the canteen and felt sick with disappointment. It was a significant setback. *'I've got to plan another attempt with more care. If I can't leave the hospital alone, it must be from the shops at the bottom of the hill. Who can I get to be the stooge to take me there, and when?'*

A chance presented itself when Dr Kirk asked an orderly, Barry, to take a letter to catch the lunchtime registered post. He said, 'Take John for the walk. The fresh air and exercise will be beneficial. It will give you both a break.'

Bruno felt his heart quickening. Now could be his chance. After a brisk walk to the Post Office, they gravitated to the small cafe next door. Bruno said, 'I'm fed up with hospital food. Let's have coffee and a bite here.'

Barry agreed, and Bruno ushered him to a table away from the window. It was a regular spot staff skived off to when running errands to the local pharmacy or for any items not kept at the hospital. Bruno remembered the toilet was off the main room, not visible from the tables, and that the back door led to an alley to give him cover when he crossed to the taxi.

The rank was empty, so Bruno took his time perusing the menu card on the table. 'I fancy the chicken soup with a roll. What about you?'

Barry wanted something more substantial. 'I've got a full shift ahead. I'll have the meat pie and mash.'
As the steaming food arrived, Bruno glanced through the window. Two taxis were waiting for passengers.

'Hey, Barry. You carry on eating. I've got to use the John.' Bruno bypassed the restroom and scooted down the alley and across the road to a waiting cab. He sat low in the back seat, and as they moved off, he shouted the address in Marple.

The taxi crawled along and stopped after a few seconds. 'Damn it. Sorry, guv. I left my wallet in the newspaper shop,' and the cabbie dashed across the road. Bruno thought they might have rumbled him again and leaned sideways on the seat. He turned his head so as not to be easily recognisable if his colleague started scouting for him.

Too engrossed in his pie and mash, Barry didn't realise for a while that Bruno hadn't returned. He checked the urinal and looked outside; another two taxis had filled the space. He went inside and paid the bill, but a quick sweep of the immediate area showed no sign of him.

'I bet he's had a funny turn in the toilet and made his way back,' he thought. So, he steadily climbed the hill, hoping to catch Bruno up.

Bruno was relieved when the cabbie returned, and they inched away into the traffic. He looked through the back window and saw his colleague striding towards the hospital.

Barry immediately went to Dr Kirk's office, and they took a quick, unfruitful drive around the village. When Bruno hadn't returned after a few hours, Dr Kirk phoned the local police. 'He's quite harmless, and I believe he's making his way to Marple. That's where he was trying to go last time.'

The police officer didn't seem worried. 'He can't come to much harm in Marple.' he joked. 'He'll probably turn up when he's done his recce, but we'll look out for him.'

The taxi dropped Bruno outside the pretty country house. He watched it speed down the road before taking tentative steps towards the gate.

Mabel's house comprised various farm buildings, and he noted someone had converted the farmhouse and stables into one residence. The well-kept gardens and the newly painted wooden gate were testimony to a loving hand.

Bruno hesitated for a moment, excited but afraid of it being a wasted journey. He recognised nothing and checked the house name on the card, Thistledown Farm. Anticipation, then fear of rejection, made him pause; his trembling hand lay on the iron latch before lifting it.

'The shadowy figure and the name Mabel resonated in his half-empty brain. I'm a dumbass; what am I doing? Suppose nobody's here? I should've asked the cab to wait.'

His legs threatened to buckle as he stepped onto the path.

Chapter 34

Amber's sharp bark startled Bruno; this curious tawny-coloured spaniel leapt onto the path and wagged a silky-plumed tail. The woman on a garden bench reading a newspaper lifted her head at the commotion.

A lump appeared in his throat as he instantly recognised the lady. He knew her. This is Mabel! He wanted to rush over to her but held onto the gate he had quickly closed to keep the dog in. When the dog was no threat, he gathered strength and willpower and walked toward the bench.

'Can I help you?' she asked and watched as the wiry stranger slowly approached her. The newspaper fell from her fingers. She couldn't move and just looked up, watching a thinner but familiar face take tentative steps until he stumbled onto the bench beside her.

She gasped and touched his arm; this was not a ghost. She cried, 'Oh my God. Bruno! What's happened to you?' Her shaky voice echoed shock waves throughout her body.

He begged piteously, 'Mabel, please tell me who I am.'

She turned to him and hugged his skeletal frame.

'You are Bruno Ponti of the American Medical Corps.'

Huge, searing sobs racked his whole body as he realised the fruitless searches were over. John Doe had disappeared.

Mabel wept with him, remembering the suffering they had all endured. Her fingers traced the red scar across his forehead into the dark hair, now speckled with white. She didn't dare ask too much as she clasped his hands and looked at his sunken cheeks; he seemed dazed and weak. She knew one thing; he was safe here and never going away again.

She was always the pragmatist and thought food and rest should come first; there was countless time for explanations. 'Come inside and let's get you something to drink. Have you eaten lunch?'

Exhausted by the recent activity, he willingly surrendered to Mabel and let himself be led into the cottage by this forceful matron he somehow trusted but didn't know why. He knew she was possibly the key to unlocking his past.

She watched him devour a layered ham sandwich and an enormous slice of jam sponge cake. She thought, *'He hadn't lost his appetite, so why is he so thin?'*

Over coffee, she asked him, 'What happened? Where have you been?'

'I know very little. I was caught up in a bombing in Manchester. They took me to Macclesfield hospital with amnesia. Only a few things seem to make sense at the moment, and I have lost a good part of my memory.'

'So, how did you find me and get yourself here?'

'Someone gave me your name, which sounded familiar, and I had to find you.'

'Well, you need look no further. This is where you're safe and you belong. I'll look after you. We'll start slowly at the beginning. Remember, your name is Bruno Ponti, and you're a medic in the American forces. I met you in my club.'

He accepted the explanation and, exhausted from the ordeal, it was only minutes before he fell asleep on the sofa, where she covered him with a rug. She kept looking at him and couldn't believe that he was actually alive and here with her. His dark skin had lost luminosity, but he was still handsome. She watched over him until dusk. The burning question filled her mind. Why had no one identified him?

Her mind was in turmoil, and more questions arose. Was Bruno in trouble? Would the police take him away? I can't risk the chance of losing him again. Crazy thoughts entered, *'If he was a dog, I could lock him in whilst I made enquiries.'*

She pondered for a while; Macclesfield Hospital was where she could start. The police should also be involved here; they might know what to do next. She turned the light on in the hall, closed the living room door and picked up the phone. Nobody was talking on her party line, so she dialled the exchange, who put her through to the police station. She decided Bruno would become her nephew to get ownership of the situation and be taken seriously.

It worked; the Police were attentive when she spoke on the phone, 'My nephew has turned up at my house and told me he is a patient at a hospital in Macclesfield. They may be looking for him.'

'Yes, Madam. What's your name and telephone number, please?'

'Mabel Evans. Marple 2801.'

'Mrs Evans, we've been informed that there is a missing John Doe. Do you feel safe in the house with him, or shall we send someone to you right away?'

'Is he dangerous?' she asked.

'They didn't say so.'

'That's good because I'm fine. We've talked, I've fed him, and he's now sleeping like a baby.'

'What's this John Doe's name?'

'Bruno Ponti. He's a Lieutenant with the American Medical Corps.'

'And he's your nephew?' he said incredulously.

'Well, not exactly, but he's going to marry my niece.' she explained. 'She's not here, and he has no relatives in England; that's why I feel responsible for his welfare.'

'Right. Fine, I think I've got the story straight. So, he's not your nephew; he's an intended and has no relatives here. We'll contact the hospital, and they'll call you back immediately.'

Within minutes, Dr Kirk called Mabel, who was still lurking in the hall, polishing the black bakelite phone. She picked it up on the first ring so as not to wake Bruno.

'Dr Kirk here. Good evening. Am I speaking to Mrs Evans?'

'Yes. Thank you for calling back. Bruno Ponti turned up at my house today, and I thought someone would be looking for him?'

Dr Kirk said, 'So his name is Bruno. We have a missing person. Is he American with a large scar on his forehead?'

'Yes, he has. Can you tell me what happened?' Mabel asked.

'I'd prefer not to discuss it on the phone. May I come and collect him?'

'Why? Is he in trouble? Do you need to take him away?'

'No, not in trouble. Let's discuss this more when I get there. Could you please give me your address?'

Mabel felt pressurised but needed to know more. She gave her address and directions, and Dr Kirk sat with her at the kitchen table within half an hour.

They looked in at the sleeping Bruno, and Mabel said, 'All I know is he just turned up today, right out of the blue.'

Dr Kirk filled in the background he knew. It's such a breakthrough that he somehow found his way here. There's obviously a strong link between you. He's been with us for about eighteen months, and we've been trying to find out who our John Doe is.'

Mabel said, 'Your John Doe is actually Lieutenant Bruno Ponti from the American Army Medical Corps. He disappeared into thin air, and his unit went to France without him. They thought he deserted until his dog tag was found months later in the rubble of a building flattened by a bomb and presumed dead.'

'He's very much alive but in awful shape mentally. How do you know him?'

'He's almost a relative of mine. He was dating my niece, Felicity, who lives with me. Can you believe it? She's in the States visiting his parents. I now feel doubly responsible for him.'

'How long have they known each other?' he asked.

'Long enough to have a baby together.' she ventured. 'But he doesn't know he's a father. I think we'll keep that surprise to ourselves for now.'

'Yes, indeed. He could only remember a few Italian folk songs and very little else. He has endeared himself to us, but we always hoped he would recover enough to leave. Sadly, some never do.'

'So, he knows nothing? Have we got to help him piece it all back together? We have some of his family photos, so we have something to start with.'

'What's his background?' Dr Kirk asked.

Mabel told him just enough to satisfy his curiosity. She didn't know too much more anyhow.

Dr Kirk beamed; he was ecstatic to know their John Doe had found his way to this lovely, caring lady who desperately wanted him back.

Mabel said, 'Does he need to go back with you? Perhaps he could continue his recovery with me under your supervision until Felicity gets home?'

'He's been no trouble at the hospital. In fact, he's been a great help on the wards. If he's happy here with you, we can give it a few days and see how you both cope. Why don't you come back to the hospital with him to collect his things, and we can discuss what's best for his further recovery.'

Mabel agreed and sat at the table in complete disbelief. She could do so many things: contact Felicity, tell his parents, and even reveal to Bruno that he has a child. Somehow, it didn't feel right to do any of them immediately.

She vowed she would try to give him back to Felicity in better shape than he was now, a cruel caricature of his old self. Her spirits lifted at thoughts of their future happiness when they reunited. She couldn't wait to let them know; they should know that he was alive. She'd have to liaise with Dr Kirk on the timing.

Bruno woke, agitated at the sound of voices. At first, he didn't recognise where he was, but he soon realised it was Dr Kirk and Mabel.

Mabel calmly said, 'Bruno, Dr Kirk's here, and I'm going to ask him if you can convalesce with me. Would you like that?

Dr Kirk looked over and softly said, 'So John Doe, you eventually have a real name, Bruno Ponti. Does that ring any bells?'

He shook his head, 'Not at the moment, but I do know this is Auntie Mabel.'

'Well, that's a good start. You found your way here without our intervention, so let's see how things progress. You can always return to the hospital if it doesn't work out. I've left my direct number.'

Bruno looked at Mabel, who was grinning from ear to ear. 'Yes, that sounds good to me, Dr Kirk.'

'OK, let's pop back to the hospital and get your things.'

Bruno asked, 'Can Mabel come too?' He wanted to hold on to this particular person.

'Of course, she can come. Let's get started.'

Mabel looked at Bruno, *'It's pitiful to see him this way. He looks uncertain and anxious and doesn't want to return to that hospital. Thankfully, this doctor seems happy enough with him and has encouraged the arrangement.'*

Dr Kirk showed them the way to his office. The bush telegraph worked overtime, and the staff soon heard of Bruno's return and lined the corridor to welcome him back. Amazed and incongruous in this austere medical environment, they watched this tall, commanding, middle-aged woman walk with Bruno holding his hand like a child.

Bruno recognised his colleagues and smiled. Without explanation, he said, 'I've come to collect my things.'

Dr Kirk introduced Mabel. 'This is Mrs Evans; she knows our John Doe.'

They were dumbstruck when she announced, 'And this is Lieutenant Bruno Ponti of the American Medical Corps. Dr Kirk has agreed that Bruno will recuperate with me for the time being.'

An orderly responded, 'No wonder he was so comfortable working with us. Funny now to think we thought he was a spy or a film star.'

Dr Kirk said, 'Yes, Bruno will stay with Mrs Evans, who will liaise with us. Will someone please take him and help pack his belongings?'

'It's actually Miss Evans but do call me Mabel.' She smiled at these caring people. 'I'll be looking forward to your visits now he has a base in Marple. I'm sure it will be helpful to his recovery, and I can tell you more about his background. Not a spy, nor a film star, but still very interesting.'

Dr Kirk studied Mabel and gave a quick resume of Bruno's medical background since admission to his office.

He said, 'So Bruno is a medic. That makes sense. He's gentle and kind with the other patients; he's been so much help on the ward and doesn't appear to have a nasty bone in his body. I think being with someone familiar might trigger more memories. You must call me if things get difficult. Here's my private number, and I will inform my staff you have it.'

They agreed that would be the way forward, and Dr Kirk rose to escort Mabel out.

Bruno was relieved and relaxed in his familiar but stark hospital surroundings. Two lads accompanied him to fill a suitcase with the few items he had accrued.

Mabel had such a capable persona. Dr Kirk almost expected his staff to bow as they left. In admiration, he chuckled, 'This woman should do my job. She'd keep them all in check.'

Dr Kirk insisted on driving them back to Marple. Mabel mentally went over the instructions. 'The first step to recovery is to make him feel safe and give him the basics. When it seems right, introduce his background, tell him about his family, and show him any photographs. Slowly, slowly. It's important to let him set the pace.'

On arrival at the cottage, Dr Kirk and Bruno lined up to open the car door for Mabel. They looked at each other, nodded, and Bruno started up the path. Dr Kirk shouted after him, 'Goodnight, Lieutenant Ponti. See you soon.'

Dr Kirk drove off satisfied, in good spirits, curious to know more about his favourite patient, not to mention an enjoyable meeting with the remarkable Aunt Mabel, who is also a Miss.

Bruno refused a nightcap inside the cottage, so Mabel led him to a bedroom.

As he turned to say goodnight, Mabel clasped his hands, 'You don't know how much today has changed our lives. Many people love you and will be so thrilled to have you back. Don't worry about a thing. You're welcome to stay as long as possible to get you well. I'll fill in some more details tomorrow. Sleep well. I'm sure you will.'

Bruno kissed her on the cheek. He still didn't know where she fitted in, but it felt right, and she seemed bowled over with happiness to be with him.

He sat on the single bed. At last, he could relax. It was a good start that he knew his real name and background. He felt at home, and the overwhelming urge to find out about himself, which dominated his time in the hospital, had disappeared in a puff of smoke. He stowed his few items into drawers, picked up and smelt the fresh, soft towel laid out for him, and crossed to the bathroom with his wash bag.

Tucked up in bed, he went over his findings. *'I've never felt so tired, but I am no longer a missing person. I am Lieutenant Bruno Ponti, an American staying with Auntie Mabel in Marple. Why do I call her Auntie?'*

Mabel popped her head in once during the night, but he remained in the same sleeping position, tired to the bone. She checked on him again at eight in the morning. He'd made the bed but was not in the room. She looked at the empty bed in horror.

Chapter 35

Bruno had awakened early to strange sounds in unfamiliar surroundings. He heard a scratching at the bedroom door and found Amber jumping in circles, leading him towards stairs and the back door, urging him to go outside. He remembered from yesterday that the dog was called Amber. Was it allowed out? She might escape.

He unlocked the door and poked his head out. The air was crisp, and he noticed the autumn leaves with their brilliant colour through the misty morning haze. Amber scrambled through his legs and immediately ran towards the bushes.

Bruno followed her and sat on the dewy wet seat in his pyjamas, savouring freedom from the hospital stench of disinfectant and carbolic. A path wound between the lawn and the late flowering borders planted with random selections, the total effect of rounded shrubs was soothing and restful.

He called Amber's name and hoped she would return. Within seconds, she came scuttling with anticipation out of the bushes. The next thing on her agenda was breakfast.

Memories of yesterday's traumatic arrival were still with him. He remembered Auntie Mabel and the little dog, and Dr Kirk knew he was safe here. Bruno walked along the path back to the house, accompanied by his newfound furry friend. 'Where are we going next?' he said as Amber led him towards an empty water bowl underneath the outside tap.

Bruno filled it, and a nudge on the arm made him jump. 'There you are.' Mabel said, hiding her relief. 'I forgot to give you a dressing gown. Let me fetch one. Come in, and we'll have breakfast. We'll take Amber for a walk, and we can explore Marple if you like?'

Over coffee in the kitchen, she noticed he was still far from lucid but was good company and willing to help. They spent the morning chatting about the chores, and she was sure not to overtire his mind with too much information. She brought out the photo of his parents. 'These are Eva and Carlo.'

Bruno took a photograph, glanced at it and exclaimed, 'Ma, Pa!'

'So, you recognise them then?'

'Yes!' With tears in his eyes, holding the photograph tightly in both hands, he looked up. 'Are they still alive, or have I forgotten?'

Mabel smiled. 'Yes, they're alive, in excellent health. They were here last month. In this house, we all thought you were missing.'

He sighed with relief, 'They live in England?'

She laughed. 'No, they travelled over from Napa.'

'Napa. California! Oh, I remember that place. Don't we have a vineyard?'

'Yes, your memory's working well today. Dr Kirk will be relieved you've remembered more. Leaving you here with me was the right thing to do. Keep asking questions; I don't mind. I'll help where I can.' She left him with the photograph of his parents, hoping it might trigger more.

Mabel was bursting to tell someone that Bruno was back from the dead. Anna was the only one in the UK who knew him and could be trusted to keep the secret. She wrote asking Anna to call her urgently as there was good news.

The following evening, Anna called from the phonebox at the end of the street. Mabel couldn't contain herself, and the words came tumbling out. 'Bruno's not dead. He turned up here yesterday afternoon.'

Anna was incredulous. 'What? Are you sure it's him?'

'Of course, I'm sure. He gave me a proper fright. I thought he was a ghost.'

'Where's he been?' Anna asked.

'In a hospital in Macclesfield for months with amnesia. They couldn't find out his background. Everywhere they tried, they pulled a blank. Somehow he found me, and he's staying here. He's got such a short memory, so we've got to put it back together slowly.'

'Does Mum know?' said Anna, excited at the prospect of her mother's delight.

'Not yet. I've promised Dr Kirk we would trickle information to Bruno and let him get back some coherence before overloading his mind with Felicity and Carl.'

'Can we visit? Do you need help while the others are away in America?'

'That would be wonderful. When can you come? I'm fit to bursting and can't tell anyone else. His mind is delicately balanced, and his memory's slowly returning, so please be ultra-careful about what you say.'

Anna said, 'We'll come over on Friday night. We'll drive up as soon as we finish here for the weekend. I can't believe it. Perhaps when I see him, I'll accept it. Are you sure it's him?'

'Stop saying that!' said Mabel.

'I can't wait! We'll be with you around ten on Friday night.'

The next day, Mabel showed Bruno a few more black-and-white photos. 'This is my niece, Anna and her new husband, Frank. When they were recently married, someone took these when we held their wonderful reception in this garden. They are keen to see you and will be here for the weekend if that's okay?'

'They look very happy. Has she red hair?' He pointed to Anna.

'Yes. Do you remember her?'

'Vaguely. Of course, I don't mind them coming; perhaps they might jog my memory.'

Anna told Frank the fantastic news, and he agreed they should visit. 'We must play it cool and follow Auntie Mabel's lead. We don't want to confuse him further.'

When Anna first saw Bruno, hiding her shock at his frail condition was difficult. She wanted to cry. Frank had never met him, so it was easier to accept this stranger and go along with the women's conversation.

Bruno stared at the couple and remembered the girl's red hair. He didn't know her husband. As soon as Bruno heard Anna's commanding voice, he relaxed, transported to another time on the fringes of his consciousness.

Mabel had primed Anna and Frank to keep the conversation on their work in Birmingham, with no reference to Felicity, Carl, or the USA. They needn't have worried; Bruno was slowly unravelling his memory and adjusting to an everyday English home life away from the hospital regime.

The next day, Mabel treated the four of them to lunch at the local inn, as no one would recognise Bruno. She was also eager to hear more about Anna and Frank's new venture in Birmingham. The factory supplied the army with rucksacks and tents during the war. After the ceasefire, Frank first lent large tents to local organisations, such as the scouts, then saw an opportunity to make a living.

Frank said, 'We manufacture larger tents and pavilions for weddings and fetes. There was no money in just lending tents and, fortunately, no competition in hiring them. We'd hit gold; this was our future niche market.'

Anna said, 'Mr Timpson agreed and gave us complete control to run this company branch. He was delighted with our foresight and reaping a good profit.' She presented them with a glossy brochure showing photographs of previous events. 'I've come a long way since using a sewing machine.' she boasted to her great aunt.

After the weekend, Mabel saw them off. 'Thank you for dropping everything and coming straight over. I feel much more relaxed now; even Bruno feels that normality is returning. I'll keep you posted.'

For Bruno, the weekend was fruitful. All this new conversation was stimulating after months of hospital monotony. As they left, Bruno embraced them with warmth naturally felt towards family.

When Dr Kirk checked up on his patient, he found a remarkable improvement. Bruno had stopped being passive and was making decisions. He advised Mabel, 'Invent ways to consult him, let him become involved in the simplest home procedures. Well done, keep up the good work.'

She thought, *'Such a lovely man; he was thrilled with Bruno's progress. He must have felt so frustrated when getting nowhere. I can see the rapport between them.'*

Bruno didn't associate her house with anything he had shared with Felicity. Marple was a long way from Ardwick Green in every way.

When Bruno's ex-colleagues arrived at the cottage with Dr Kirk, he first showed them the garden. Mabel had arranged a table outside for tea and proudly displayed her homemade cherry cake. She thought, 'They wouldn't get that in the hospital.'

It was a welcome bridge for Bruno between the two worlds. He questioned nothing and lived for the moment. Whenever Dr Kirk knew the lads were planning to visit Bruno, he dropped them there in his car on a pretext to check on his patient and took the opportunity to spend an hour with the fascinating Mabel.

This strategy allowed Mabel and the doctor to enjoy a stress-free time together, giving him a break from the spartan hospital life. There was plenty to find out about each other - an unlikely liaison under any condition.

Mabel couldn't believe how settled and happy Bruno had become in such a short time. This was due in part to Amber, who had found a replacement playmate. He had learned to relax by throwing the ball in the garden and brushing her silky fur ready for their daily walk.

Mabel noticed the grubbiness of Bruno's light jacket, whereas all the rest of his few clothes had been through the hospital laundry and while preparing to wash it, she emptied the pockets. There was only a handkerchief and a business card belonging to Bill Briggs, her friend. Her address on the back was puzzling so she rang him.

Bill said, 'I remember giving my last grubby card to an American. I found him outside our club. We got chatting andI told him that Mabel and I had founded the club. He remembered the name, described you and asked for your address. I thought he was on holiday and presumed he would send you a postcard from The States. What's happened?'

'Can we meet up, Bill and I'll fill you in? I'll also treat you to some new business cards!'

Mabel now had an valid excuse to phone Dr Kirk. 'I've got our missing link of how Bruno found me. It was in his jacket pocket. Why don't you bring the boys here tomorrow.'

She thought, *What an amazing coincidence. This is more than fate taking an interest.*

As the days progressed, Mabel brought out more family photographs that Eva and Carlo had left with Felicity. They had initially brought them to show the Cavallo's, written on the back were names. Little did the Ponti's know, but these snaps would be instrumental in recovering their son's mental health.

Dr Kirk was so pleased with Bruno's progress that he agreed Mabel could telephone Bruno's parents. She took a deep breath, dialled the exchange, and gave them the long international number. She hadn't checked the time difference but guessed it must be mid-morning over there. With her news, it would never matter what time it was.

Chapter 36

Mabel was bubbling over with excitement. 'Hello, Carlo? This is Mabel from England. How are you?'

'Hi, Mabel. Lovely to hear from you. All's well here. How are things with you?'

Mabel said firmly, almost shouting as the line was quite faint, 'Carlo, please remember every word I tell you so you can pass it on to Eva. I have wonderful news.'

'Of course. What's this good news?' He could hear the strength and excitement in her voice.

'Bruno, your darling son, is alive and with me. He's not missing and certainly not dead. Repeat this to me; I want to ensure you've got it.'

'Are you kidding?' In a quivery voice, Carlo said slowly, 'Bruno is alive and with you.' The line went quiet, but Mabel heard stifled sobs from the man on the other end.

Mabel reiterated, 'Are you still there? I know it's a shock; I couldn't believe it either.'

Carlo composed himself enough to ask, 'What happened? Where's he been? Can I talk to him?'

'He's sleeping at the moment, but I must tell you he's in pretty poor shape mentally. You know that building site you visited? He was caught up in that bombing and taken to hospital. He lost his memory; that's why we didn't hear from him.'

'Really. So that's what happened. Does he remember us over here?'

'Yes. He does now. He's still fragile, and his doctor advised me to trickle information to him. We couldn't gauge how well-balanced his mind was, so we were careful the past three weeks he's been with me. He had a lot to assimilate.'

'Three weeks! And you didn't tell us.' Carlo sounded angry.

'I knew you'd be cross and I'm so sorry. It's been awful, and I often wanted to pick up the phone, but I was under Dr Kirk's strict instructions.'

Carlo's voice softened, 'Okay. What else can you tell us?' She relayed everything she knew.

Carlo sighed, 'So he's physically intact, no missing limbs?'

'No, he's still skinny, quiet, and happy to be out of the hospital. The entire story is staggering; he turned up here after eighteen months. Something must have triggered a memory. You know how far I am from central Manchester. I still can't fathom out how he found me.'

'I'm sure it will all become clear at some time.'

'Carlo, why don't you telephone us back later today? I'll prime him that you'll be calling. He knows very little at the moment. He recognises you both from the photographs and recalls the vineyard. Speaking to you may jog his memory a little more.'

'Wait until I tell Eva. She's going to have one helluva shock.'

'By the way, please don't mention Carl or Felicity. We haven't got that far in his recovery.'

'Oh, you haven't. Boy, this is serious. Shall we tell Felicity?'

'Yes, please. But tell her it will be a long process, but I'm confident he'll return to his old self in time. Call anytime, even if it's the middle of the night for you. When you tell Eva, I wish I were a fly on the wall.'

He laughed, 'In the next few minutes, if you hear a high shriek over there in England, you'll know I've told her!'

Carlo stood up and walked towards the closed study door but couldn't open it immediately. Not able to face Eva yet, he slumped in the nearest chair, put his head in his hands, and sobbed. Relief and joy were overpowering. He never expected this call, and his overwhelming love for his poor son was gut-wrenching.

He took a few minutes to digest the news and marched, head held high, into the kitchen. Eva was chopping vegetables for that evening's dinner. She stopped when she saw his face, blotchy and tear-stained.

'What's the heck's up?' she asked.

He shook his head. 'Nothing bad. I have amazing news. Come and sit next to me.'

She wiped her hands on a tea towel and strolled over to the kitchen table. Carlo held her hand as she sat facing him. 'Mabel just called from England, and they've found Bruno alive.'

Eva gasped, and it took a millisecond for her to comprehend what he'd told her.

'Oh My God. Alive. Bruno,' she cried.

'He's with Mabel. He got amnesia from the bomb blast, and he's been in hospital all this time.'

'Tell me everything she told you.' Eva said, tears dropping onto her lap.

As they hugged, they shed pent-up grief in the rare and emotional "Thank you, God" moment. They were utterly shocked; they couldn't find anything but weeping to express their profound, raw emotions.

Eva kept crossing herself and raising her eyes to heaven. She repeated 'Grazie' so many times as Carlo sat back in his chair. It was unbelievable, and he stared for ages with so much love at his overjoyed wife, still crossing herself and thanking Dio and any saint that came to mind.

When Eva stopped wailing, Carlo said, 'He hasn't been told about Felicity or Carl yet, but we can tell Felicity we have found him. I think we need Tony and Franco here first.'

Eva agreed, and Carlo hurried over to the office. Within minutes Tony turned up. Franco decided first to call in on Susan and tell her.

Franco called out, 'You'll never believe it. Bruno's alive and kicking in England.'

Susan said, 'Is that right? Where's he been then?'

'In the hospital with amnesia. This changes everything. Forget about the inheritance, blood tests, all of it.'

'It's your brother they've found. Aren't you the least bit happy about it?'

'Not really. I'm pushed back to second place again.'

Susan couldn't believe what she heard, and wondered what sort of man she had married.

'I've got to go over to Ma's. They're going to tell Felicity. It'll be interesting to see her reaction.'

Eva and Carlo were so full of joy to bring the news that Felicity and Betsy heard animated chattering well before the four approached the front door. Carlo didn't need to press the doorbell as she opened it before they reached the top step. They were beaming, and Felicity wondered what on earth they were up to.

She smiled back. 'Come in. From your faces, it looks like this is a nice social visit. Would you like some coffee?'

Betsy shouted from the kitchen, 'Good morning, everyone,' and then joined them in the sitting room.

Eva took Felicity's hands, 'We have some wonderful news. I think you'll want to sit down.'

Felicity felt uneasy, looked at Betsy, but obeyed the instruction as she looked around at their animated faces. Eva looked her in the eyes and couldn't help the tears as she blurted out, 'They've found Bruno! Alive!'

To everyone's infinite disappointment and surprise, there were no wild expressions of delight and utter joy from Felicity, just total disbelief.

She shouted, 'No! This is too much. It's a cruel, practical joke. It's not true.' She jumped up and paced up and down the room. 'Where is he then? It's all lies, all lies!' Tears poured down her face. 'I've grieved for him, and he is dead. Dead!' she screamed and became hysterical, seemed to lose all reason, and sat on the floor, drumming her heels like a child, sobbing bitterly.

The onlookers were astounded and didn't quite know what to do. They looked from one to the other, and Betsy rushed over to comfort her mother. Franco nipped into the hall and called the local doctor, who arrived within minutes. Tony took Carl by the hand and called Gina to come to Bruno's house quickly.

The doctor was apprised of the background to the histrionics and stayed with Felicity. The others retired to the kitchen, and after fifteen minutes, he walked in, 'The news was a profound shock, and I've sedated her. She's lying on the sofa, and I'll call round later to check on her progress.'

Gina arrived mystified, and Tony said, 'Can you look after Carl? Felicity has taken some news badly and may be sedated for a while. I'll fill you in later.' Carl left with Gina and was happy to walk around the corner and play with the big boy's toys.

Franco stood helplessly, watching Felicity, who seemed to relive Bruno's death, unable to cope with another let-down. Compassion swept through him. He thought, *This is not a chancer G.I. bride, but a poor bereft woman reacting to stress. She really loved him.* He then started thinking of publicity. *'The locals, friends, and the press turned up in droves at the memorial. How much more of a story have they got now? They would be ecstatic.'*

Betsy stayed with her mother, initially elated at the news, then terrified by her mother's reaction. She'd never seen her like this.

Eva made an urgent telephone call to Mabel. 'We're bowled over by the news, but Felicity has gone into shock. She didn't believe it and went into a screaming fit. So bad she had to be sedated by the doctor. Can you come over a little earlier? She really needs to see Bruno in the flesh.'

Mabel said, 'Leave it to me. I'll call you back tomorrow. I'll contact Dr Kirk and see what he says about Bruno travelling such a long way.'

She glanced over at Bruno, riffling through the daily newspaper. On the sideboard were the photographs of his family lined up on display. She phoned Dr Kirk. 'Such a lot has happened. Felicity was told Bruno was alive, and she flipped with shock. She had to be sedated and won't believe it until she sees him. It means we've lost a week of grace, but I think I should take him over sooner. I hope all this won't set him back.'

Dr Kirk said, 'If he were going to flip, it would have happened by now. He's very resilient. Now the practicalities. Go to the travel agent and let me know the dates. Jimmy can move into your house to look after Amber. He loves her, and I'll drop him off the day before.'

'That would be such a relief. I'm so grateful to leave Amber in good hands.'

Dr Kirk said, 'Bruno will need to come back sometime to see me for an assessment. There's still one thing that mystifies me. How on earth did he find his way to you? What was the trigger? You might find out. It would be good for our records.'

'I'll try to find out for you. I agree, in his state, it's quite remarkable.'

She felt guilty. *'Fancy forgetting Amber. Thank goodness Dr Kirk is on the ball. Bruno will stay longer, so I'll pack enough for a week.'*

A couple of days later, Mabel sat beside Bruno at the kitchen table, 'How would you like to take a trip to Napa next week?'

He looked anxious, so she said, 'It's okay, Dr Kirk has signed you off. Your family desperately want to see you, and Felicity is there visiting them.'

He said, 'Felicity' as though he was practising the name. Something cranked up in his mind.
Mabel said, 'Yes, my niece, which is why you're staying with me until she gets back.'

'Let me run through this with you. I know you're Auntie Mabel, and Felicity's your niece. Anna, her daughter, was here with Frank, and Anna has a blonde sister; what's her name?'

'Betsy. I'll get the photographs.'

'No need. I know them. I can see them,' he shouted in triumph. His face lit up, transfixed, as their faces appeared through the mists of his memory. He suddenly stood up, holding onto the table's edge. He looked down at Mabel. 'Oh my God. I remember Felicity.' He tapped his head. 'My darling Felicity has been locked in here all this time.'

Mabel staggered up and hugged him with relief at the end of the subterfuge. She couldn't help but join in with tears of joy.

During the day, Mabel brought a photograph of Felicity. Bruno's brain fog lifted to reveal more memories of her and his enormous feelings. He plunged into action and hurried over to the phone, 'Mabel, I want to phone Felicity now to tell her I'm coming over.'

'No, I'm sorry, Bruno, but you can't just yet. Your family are telling her gently today that you're alive and here with me. It will no doubt come as a great shock. I remember vividly the moment you came through my gate, and I thought you were a ghost. It's a good job I have a strong heart. She'll be used to the news by the time we get there.' Mabel didn't want to say, 'She's currently having hysterics and in complete denial.'

She said, 'But I can now give you more photos of her. It's a long flight to our first stop, New York; I'll fill in the details then.'

He picked another photo and traced Felicity's features with his fingertips, pressed the picture quickly to his lips, and clutched it tightly while he wandered around the room, willing his mind to remember more. 'Felicity! How on earth could I have forgotten her? I knew we should be together from the first moment I met her. She felt it too.'

Mabel watched the transformation and mentally stored everything for Dr Kirk's notes. 'But Bruno, your mind shut down everything. You even had to learn to speak. When you came here, you barely recognised me; you didn't know who I was or where I fit in.'

Bruno's face lit up after this conversation, and he couldn't stop smiling as relief flooded his body. He had spent months in despair of ever finding his identification and memory. Today it was as though somebody had thrown open the blackout curtains, and a beautiful colourful world was beckoning him to step outside.

Chapter 37

Felicity and Betsy waited for Mabel and Bruno in the arrivals hall at San Francisco airport, supported by Eva and Carlo.

Betsy said, 'Are you feeling better, Mum? Carl will be fine; Gina's looking after him upstairs, watching the planes come in.'

Eva clasped Felicity's hand and squeezed it with excitement. 'Bruno will come through that door in a few minutes.'

Jolted out of her mental fog, Felicity whispered, 'Bruno's alive. It is true!'

Afraid of another bout of hysteria, Eva said, 'Let's stand up, and we'll be the first people he sees as he comes through.'

Eva and Betsy came forward and clasped Felicity's elbows in case her legs buckled.

Bruno and Mabel appeared like a conjuring trick in the doorway. He marched straight to Felicity and enveloped her in his arms. Her face pressed hard into his chest, and as she tilted her face upwards, she gasped for air. He wanted to explore each of her features and kissed around her face until he became breathless.

He held her at arm's length and looked at her flushed pink face; her hair shone golden in the stark overhead lights. 'Beautiful Felicity,' he whispered. She held onto his hands to remind her he was real and alive and loved her. She let go suddenly, only to fling her arms around him and sob into his shoulder.

Bruno looked over her head at his stunned family and moved over to his parents and brothers. Only when he said, 'Hi folks.' Did they believe he was real? There was a sudden clamour when they all spoke at once, laughing, crying and hugging. Bruno lifted his mother triumphantly. Carlo then shook his hand and brought him into the biggest hug. Betsy broke away from the tearful scene, eager to embrace her precious great-aunt standing apart from the group.

Carlo followed her and clasped Mabel's hands looking steadily into her eyes. He said, 'Dear, dear Mabel, how can we ever thank you enough? First, you lifted us from deep sorrow and led us to our grandson, then nurtured our injured son and brought him back safely to us.'

Eva came in on this sincere declaration and, speechless, hugged Mabel, and pressed her head on her shoulder, which left the coat tear-stained.

Passengers hurried by and gave them curious glances, guessing something momentous was happening.

Still clinging to each other, the family propelled them to the nearby cafe. There were no words to express their emotions on such a momentous occasion. To hug, laugh, and weep with joy was enough.

Felicity and Bruno sat down and leaned against each other, fatigue etched on their faces.

Mabel looked at Bruno, 'When you left, your instructions were, "Look after Felicity for me." How ironic, and what a reversal, that I should find myself looking after you for her.' She heaved a sigh of relief and said, 'I can relax now. My duty has been done.'

Carlo fetched Gina and the toddler. Felicity took the boy's hand and turned to Bruno. 'Bruno, meet your son, Carl.'

He looked at Felicity, then at the boy. He didn't understand, knew nothing about a boy; was this another thing his mind had forgotten?

Felicity said, 'I found out I was pregnant after you'd disappeared.'

Bruno accepted her explanation, crouched to Carl's level, and smiled. He stared at the boy, taking in and devouring every detail of his face; somehow, the features were already familiar. This walking replica was indeed his son. He turned to look at Felicity with such love that everybody blinked away tears for fear of upsetting the child.

Eva and Carlo took Carl home while two shocked and damaged people, Bruno and Felicity, went home to rest. They insisted on walking alone around the corner to Bruno's house. Dusk had just fallen. Felicity felt shy as she tucked her arm in his, and they set off slowly. Bruno stopped suddenly. She couldn't see his face.

'What is it?' she asked.

'I've got to say it. I feel shell-shocked, catapulted through the last month. Suddenly I have found you and a darling son, but I still haven't been able to slot into this new body. At the hospital, I longed to know who I was, and I realise I'm lucky to have this part of my memory back. I'm worried that people could ask too much of me, and I don't want to disappoint anyone. I still don't feel like me. It's as if I've inherited a new persona.'

She moved from his side and stood before him, grasping his hands. 'I'm glad you're brave enough to share your doubts with me. So much has happened to both of us. We are not the same couple who went to Blackpool and discussed sharing a life. We've missed out on our courtship. We're a ready-made couple with a house and a child, but we are both still in shock. At least we've been honest, which is a great first step. We don't have to sleep with each other simply because it's expected.'

He let her hands go, put his arms around her back and stopped the impassioned words with a kiss. Her lips were trembling. Then a warmth flooded him, and he covered her face with more kisses. He held her up, and half carried her the short distance to the house.

They stumbled into the hall. He dared to switch on the light, and they looked at each other. Tears were trickling down her face.

He said, 'There are no rules in this unusual relationship. No timelines. One thing I know for sure, I love you, my darling, and I want to spend the rest of my life with you. We knew it then, and for me, nothing has changed.'

Her legs gave way, and she plopped down on the hall chair. He chuckled and dashed off, returning with glasses in one hand and a bottle of champagne that he had found lurking in the back of the fridge in the other.

Felicity said, 'Let's drink to us.'

Bruno raised his glass. 'To us. We'll have to get to know each other all over again.'

He led her along the hall with a wicked chuckle. 'Your room or mine?'

'Does it matter?' she smiled, realising the attraction for both of them was still alive, 'Plenty of rooms to choose from and loads of time to spend in them.'

Gina and Tony took Betsy and Carl back to their house. Only when they saw Bruno could they believe the incredible story. They stayed up late chatting about the day's momentous happening.

Mabel stayed with Eva and Carlo. They could all relax; this had been a rollercoaster year. Mabel had helped to restore their son to them. They sat quietly together, remembering their visit to her when they tried to trace Felicity.

Eva said, 'I've always wondered, would you have let us go without telling us Felicity was your niece, and their baby was asleep in the next room? I'll never rest until I know.'

'Good question,' Mabel said, 'At first, I didn't wish to tell you, but I knew I had to. You were so sad and searching for anything to lift your spirits. I thought just finding Felicity, knowing Bruno had spent his leave with her, would be enough for you, but Carl had brightened all our lives, and you deserved to know he existed. While I was absorbed in this enormous dilemma, I knew he was the tangible link to help you heal. However, fate intervened and brought Felicity back early, so she was the one to decide.' She wiped away a tear. 'I'm getting soft in my old age. I've wept more in the past couple of years than in the rest of my life.'

They laughed, and Carlo said, 'Ah! But this time, they are tears of joy.'

Chapter 38

Bruno and Felicity spent a few days adjusting to each other and new surroundings. All those barren months in the hospital, were followed by multiple discoveries; first an identity, then his true love, but the greatest gift was a newfound son. He had resigned himself to a childless life, content to enjoy nephews and their progress. The utter joy of experiencing a son would always remain fresh in his heart. The family soon accepted their presence, which seemed natural and perfect. The couple acknowledged that their enforced separation lurked in their backgrounds, reminding them that life is fragile and they should enjoy and appreciate every moment.

He never tired of incredulous family members and villagers, not trusting their vision, wanting to touch his arm tentatively to confirm it was not a dream; he was really alive.

One morning, Felicity reached into the bedside cabinet, 'I almost forgot. This is yours.' She handed him the gold-plated dog tag on the chain. He hardly took in the object's significance until he recognised it.

'Wow! It's my number, my dog tag. How on earth did you get it? Why's it covered in gold?'

Felicity relayed how the surveyor found it by chance, and that was why everyone presumed he was dead. She stressed how meaningful it was for the family to have something of his that had survived the bomb blast.

Bruno turned it round and round in his hands and handed it back to Felicity. He shook his head, 'I never want to wear it again.' To lighten the conversation, he added, 'Besides, I'm not a gold chain-wearing type of guy.'

She laughed and confided to him, 'I've never worn it and would prefer to give it back to your mother; she really treasured it.' The dog tag evoked many distasteful memories for both of them. Delighted with their decision, she replaced it in the drawer, and they settled further down in the bed and cuddled, knowing they wanted nothing more but each other.

He smiled to himself; he already had a surprise for Felicity; to name the next Ponti vintage after her, the love of his life.

The End

About The Author

Wendy J. Woodcock and Winifred Rowland

About Wendy J. Woodcock

Wendy is a graduate of the Open University with a BSc. Hons degree specialising in technology and advanced creative writing. She lives in Guernsey one of the UK Channel Islands with her husband, mother, mother-in-law, Burmese cat and a rescue labradoodle.
She was employed in International banking in London, then as a translator in Northern Italy and Switzerland. After moving to the UK for ten years, joining the fast developing computer software and hardware businesses, she returned home. After a couple of decades in the offshore finance industry, specialising in Trust and Compliance, she retired and looks after her mother and mother-in-law.
Her debut work, Horseshoe Bay, is an autobiography of her mother, Winifred Rowland. It was an unexpected, but fun collaboration and the wartime romance novel, The Golden Dog Tag swiftly followed. When Wendy's not writing, travelling with her husband, day trading or trying out the latest app, you can find her walking their dog on the island's beaches.

About Winifred Rowland

Winifred Rowland moved from Manchester to Guernsey in the Channel Islands in 1959 with her husband and young children. She lived a few yards from the beach and battled to create a seaside garden on sandy soil in her spare time.
Much later in life, she became an accidental author, after writing some family history stories for relatives. Her autobiography, Horseshoe Bay, was a collaboration with her eldest daughter, Wendy J. Woodcock. It takes you on the uplifting journey from a poor city

upbringing to a seaside island idyll.

Winifred combines her newfound passion of writing with gardening, depending on the season or the weather. She lives with Wendy and hosts mentally stimulating weekly bridge sessions with her second daughter, Stephanie. Her multi-talented son, Darius, an airline pilot, lives in England.

Fuelled with enthusiasm for writing, further books are in the pipeline.

Books By This Author

Horseshoe Bay

By Winifred Rowland With Wendy J. Woodcock

An Autobiography of Kindness, Joy, and Unexpected Delight.

Follow 93-year-old Winifred Rowland's insightful recollections as she entertains us with wisdom, love, and humour. From humble Manchester squalor, she brings alive her view of history, through childhood WWII evacuation to present-day Covid-19 lockdown. Despite scars from haphazard schooling, she's determined to grab an education.

Later, fate whisks her and her eccentric husband to a tiny, scenic Channel Island, where they raise their children steps from an idyllic sandy horseshoe bay.
Missing family, she compares her old vibrant post-war city life to new quirky island traditions. But soon, sun-baked summers and colourful beach activities overcome her longing, and she wonders if it's possible to reciprocate the kindness and generosity of these islanders.
Jolly jaunts to relatives in Italy and Australia will intrigue and have you trotting all over the globe. However, an astrological aspect shoots a recurrent warning to savour any happiness because it may not last. When many close relationships prematurely end, how does she confront her lifelong blight?

Intimate, engaging, and moving; this remarkable story of an exceptional and inspirational woman will pique your curiosity and reveal we are not always in control of our destiny.

Printed in Great Britain
by Amazon

15961859R00119